The ~~~~)

of the

GOLDICOOT

Dawn Treacher

Cloud Cuckoo

www.dawntreacher.com
www.facebook.com/DawnTreacherAuthor

Cloud Cuckoo Publishing, UK

First published in Great Britain in 2020 by
Cloud Cuckoo Publishing, North Yorkshire

www.dawntreacher.com

ISBN: 978-1-83853-745-6

For my husband Miles, and our daughter, Clare,
for all their support.

Chapter 1

22nd March 1897

...Despite a thick land fog, I made my second sighting of the goldicoot as it perched in a goo-goo tree. Its wings were gold in colour but for two prominent feathers, which were turquoise, matching the crest upon its head. It made no sound but alighted before I got within six feet of it. It left behind droppings, the colour of burnished copper, the size of marbles...

Polly re-read her father's last journal entry. The lower part of the page was torn, teeth marks making the last line difficult to read. The paper was singed at the edges. She closed the leather-bound journal, pushing it away from her. Whatever people were saying, she knew her father wasn't a liar. The goldicoot did exist, it had to. His journal wasn't wrong. He may have been eccentric enough to have been expelled from the Royal Ornithological Society but Polly was sure her father, Professor Wimpole Gertram, had not only seen the goldicoot but had been close to catching it. Why else would he be missing in the depths of the Hibrodean rainforest, where the mud swamps belched and the Miodine orchid could swallow bats whole, even Basu monkeys if they ventured too near?

Polly sat in her father's chair, the green leather cracked,

the armrests' wooden scrolls ending in the head of a bird, each chair leg a claw clasping a wooden sphere. Polly's feet didn't touch the ground. She picked up her father's silver fountain pen, which sat next to a bottle of emerald green ink. She remembered him sitting here just a month ago, excited at the prospect of proving them all wrong. The members of the Royal Society had laughed at the notion that the goldicoot was anything more than a mythological bird, a legend that only the insane would pursue. A tear rolled down Polly's cheek. Why couldn't Mundle remember anything? She had never liked her father's assistant. Never trusted a man whose skinny white neck didn't seem strong enough to carry the weight of his bulbous head with its bush of curls that hung so annoyingly over his eyes. Polly's aunt, Madam Grunger, said he had been found walking, dazed, in the rain forest, his feet bare and his trousers in tatters. On his calf was a six inch scratch, the claw marks of what looked like a wild cat. Mundle's spectacles were smashed and he was dehydrated and incoherent. All that remained of Polly's father, it seemed, was his journal.

Polly swivelled the chair around, taking in the shelves that reached up to the ceiling, containing the stuffed bodies of birds, each captured under a glass dome, the birds' eyes replaced by painted glass. Beside her, her father's specimen cabinet stood six feet tall. Each mahogany drawer contained eggs, carefully laid out, their name written beneath in loopy emerald green ink, a specimen feather beside it.

The door to the study creaked open. Madam Grunger filled the frame, her three chins crushing the purple chiffon ruff around her neck, her glasses hanging on a gold chain over her cumbersome bust. She narrowed her grey eyes at Polly, tapping the wooden door frame with her polished nails.

"I'd like to visit Mundle," said Polly, pre-empting her Aunt, who wasn't really her Aunt at all, of course.

"They won't take kindly to visitors at the hospital." Madam Grunger bustled over towards Polly, slamming down a newspaper on the desk, opening it at page two.

...The hunt for the mythical goldicoot ends in the suspected death of Professor Wimpole Gertram...

"Suspected," said Polly, stabbing the word. "He's not dead. Somehow Mundle must know that. He may be able to tell me something."

Madam Grunger sucked her teeth. "You may go, on the understanding that your visit will be for no longer than five minutes. Touch nothing and try not to breath too much, you never know what you might catch there."

Madam Grunger was obsessed with cleanliness. She insisted on wearing gloves when dusting specimen jars, just in case she caught a deadly disease. Good, thought Polly, at least she wouldn't want to escort her to the hospital.

"If there is no sign of your father by the end of the month,

3

arrangements will need to be made."

"Arrangements? What kind of arrangements?" said Polly.

"Well, I can't be expected to manage the house and you on my own. And I don't endure this life for love alone, either."

"If money is what you're worried about, then leave," said Polly. "I can manage alone. Father and I always could."

Madame Grunger snatched up the newspaper.

"I've written to your Uncle, Colonel Briskett, but he's away on a business trip, it seems. Too bad, he would instil some order around here at least."

Polly shuddered. The last time she had met her Uncle, her father's eldest and only surviving brother, it had been at her mother's funeral. Sandwich crumbs became wedged in his moustache, so that every time he spoke, crumbs shot across the room like ammunition. Polly never knew where to look, as one eye looked in a completely different direction than the other. No, Polly had no intention of letting Colonel Briskett move in and she doubted he would agree to it anyway. He had already made it known that he found children a disgusting nuisance. No, she was determined to find her father. She would make Mundle remember, she had to. And the journal, all that was left of her father, must contain some clues.

*

The hospital smelt of starch and death. The matron, her perfectly white apron straining across her generous midriff, escorted Polly into a white-washed ward. A row of metal beds

4

lined one wall, a small window looking out over a neatly trimmed lawn, where no weed dared to linger. When Polly saw Mundle, she almost didn't recognise him. His eyes had shrunk back inside his enormous head into deep grey hollows. His neck looked scrawnier than ever and now seemed unable to support his head, which lolled onto one side, dribble running down his chin. His body was barricaded into the bed by starched sheets, his arms lifeless by his side. The only movement was a flicker of his eyelids when Polly sat down and whispered his name.

"Mundle, it's Polly."

Nothing.

"Five minutes, no more. My patient needs his rest." With that the matron left, tapping the watch clipped to her apron.

"Mundle, where's my father?"

Mundle's lips opened, then closed, but no words escaped.

"What happened?" said Polly. Maybe Matron was right, maybe he had no memory at all.

Mundle raised one finger. It seemed to be beckoning her closer. Polly leaned in.

"A beast."

"What do you mean, a beast?" said Polly.

"It...took...him." These last few words rasped from Mundle's lips. Then he fell silent. His eyes closed, his fingers now motionless once more.

"A beast took my father? What beast?"

5

But Mundle lay like a ghost, swallowed now by his sheets.

"Time you were leaving." Matron ushered Polly out of the ward and escorted her to the main entrance.

"As I warned you, he has no memory of what happened. We can only wait now, but I don't hold out much hope. Don't waste your time coming again, it won't help him."

Chapter 2

The carriage rattled down Maybridge Crescent, away from the hospital and towards the centre of Pringleton. Polly sat watching out of the window, as the dappled mare trotted along the cobbles, their coachman hunched over the reins, his white breeches tucked into tall black boots. Madam Grunger sat beside her, her ample bottom squashing Polly up against the carriage door.

"Well I told you he wouldn't remember anything. I hope you scrubbed your hands before leaving."

"You're wrong," said Polly, pulling down the window to let the spring air waft inside, bringing with it the smell of blossom. "Mundle said my father was taken by a beast."

"Delirium," said Madam Grunger, delving into a paper bag of peppermints and popping one into her mouth. "Exploring can make a man mad, so they say, and no wonder, walking in the rainforest with no water, no rest from the sun."

Polly remembered the scratches on Mundle's calf. A beast. What kind of beast would live in the Hibrodean rainforest, thought Polly. Mundle wasn't delirious, Polly was sure of that. He was haunted, haunted by something he had seen and whatever it was, it was connected with her father's disappearance, it had to be.

"I shan't allow you to visit Mundle again," said Madam

Grunger, her breath so minty that it made Polly's eyes water.

"The matron thinks he may never recover," said Polly. She wished she knew what Mundle had seen. Her father's journal made no mention of a beast.

"Let that be an end of it," said Madam Grunger. She leaned across Polly, reaching for the window to close it, her voluminous sleeve rubbing up against Polly's nose.

"Leave it," said Polly, stifling a sneeze. "I love the smell of the pavements after the rain."

"The dampness makes my bones complain," said Madam Grunger, crunching the peppermint loudly.

They were passing the tall iron gates of the city zoo. Its red brick walls stood eight feet high and ran the length of the street. On a brick pillar was nailed a wooden notice board, bearing the picture of the zoo's owner, Pruella Trimbleton. Pasted across the bottom was a poster.

For Sale – All Enquiries within

"About time that filthy place was closed down." Madam Grunger had successfully shut the window and was now rummaging in her maroon carpet bag, so spacious that Polly imagined it would hold all of Madam Grunger's possessions and still have room for more. The bag took up most of the floor beneath their seat and rested up against Polly's stockinged legs, making her ankles itch. Madam Grunger refused to travel anywhere without it.

"Here it is." Madam Grunger retrieved a newspaper. She spread it out across her knees and began to read: "Dwindling visitor numbers sees city zoo forced to sell. The proprietor, Pruella Trimbleton, says she is confident the zoo's fortunes can be restored. When asked why so many of her exhibits had died recently, Pruella Trimbleton refused to comment…"

Polly remembered her father taking her to the zoo. The birds were housed in cages barely three feet wide, preventing flight. They existed solely to be gawked at. Polly couldn't bear the empty look in their eyes.

"It's a wonder any of them survive at all," said Polly. "I hope whoever buys it sets the birds free. That's what Father would have done." Polly remembered the Kildermare, a bird so rare that only six mating pairs remained in the wild, that is until Pruella Trimbleton stuffed a pair in a cage for all to see.

"Well your father was in no position to criticise," said Madam Grunger. "All those stuffed birds, full of disease and he expected me to dust them. Filthy."

"Father never killed a bird in his life," said Polly. "He loved them. His specimens were already dead when he found them."

"Really," said Madam Grunger, puckering her lips as if she had sucked a lemon. "How naive you really are. Now he is gone, I can have a good clear out."

"Father's not gone, don't say that, don't even think it."

When they arrived back in Thicket Street, Polly stepped

9

out of the carriage outside the white stone terrace that was her home. Before she had reached their green front door she knew something wasn't right. The burgundy velvet curtains that hung at her father's study window were pulled closed. Polly knew she'd left them open. She had popped in early that morning to find a map and had opened them herself.

Madam Grunger fumbled the key, her bust heaving with the effort. When at last the door was open, Polly pushed past her and ran down the hallway, her shoes clattering along the black and green chequered tiles.

"Rudeness, young lady, will get you nowhere in a hurry," grunted Madam Grunger, dropping her carpet bag to the floor. The door to Father's study stood open.

"We've been burgled!" cried Polly.

The drawers of her father's desk were pulled open, their contents ransacked and spilt over the floor. Papers were strewn across the desk, now soaked in emerald green ink where the ink bottle had been upturned.

"There's nothing in there worth stealing," said Madam Grunger, bursting into the room, crushing several egg shells under her feet. The specimen cabinet had also been opened, the eggs dislodged. Feathers littered the floor.

"My pearls!" cried Madam Grunger, leaving as quickly as she had arrived, tearing down the hall and climbing the stairs. "Aunt Edith's brooch. I knew it was unlucky, why else could she lose three husbands?"

Polly doubted the burglar had jewels in mind when he or she broke in. Oh no, Polly was sure it was something of her father's that the burglar was seeking and now she too ran up the stairs, overtaking Madam Grunger on the landing before darting into her own bedroom. Something told Polly that her father's journal was important, too important to leave lying around. Her chest of drawers had also been plundered, her undergarments and pinafores lay on the floor, but Polly's eyes shot across to her old doll's house that stood below the window. The wooden town house was undisturbed, its red roof tiles rather dusty, considering Madam Grunger complained she did too much housework. Inside the rooms, the miniature furniture was still laid out, with a porcelain tea set on the mahogany dining table. But no-one lived there any more, the wooden dolls had long since gone, in their place, a cobweb and a lone spider. Polly lifted the roof and there lay her father's journal, untouched, just as she had left it that morning.

"Oh thank goodness, the brooch is still here, curse and all," said Madam Grunger.

Polly could hear her heading along the corridor. She put back the roof of the doll's house and ran to her door to meet her aunt.

"There's nothing missing in father's study either." said Polly. "But they were looking for something."

"Well they missed a prize when they left your mother's

ring behind. I'd better check the silver."

Madam Grunger headed back downstairs in the direction of the dining room. The ring was the only thing left of Polly's mother, since Madam Grunger insisted on clearing out her mother's things just six months after the funeral. Polly was too young to remember much about that time but her father had insisted the ring be kept for Polly, when she was old enough.

It occurred to Polly that they hadn't established how the burglar had got in. Downstairs in the dining room, Madam Grunger counted the silver teaspoons. Polly went into the hall, down to the end and opened the door to the kitchen. The window above the butler sink had been smashed and the kitchen floor sparkled with slivers of glass like confetti on a pavement after a wedding. A trail of muddy footprints walked across the stone floor but, curiously, stopped by the doorway to the hall. Men's footprints, thought Polly, judging by the size. She picked her way across the kitchen and peered out of the broken window. The flower bed below had been trampled, a terracotta flower pot overturned and smashed on the path, as if someone had left in a hurry.

"As if I didn't have enough to do already," said Madam Grunger, standing in the doorway, leaning her substantial bulk up against the frame. "Of course, the constabulary will have to be called." Madam Grunger visibly sagged, her extra chins like deflated tyres supporting her neck. Even her chest seemed to droop.

"I'll make tea," said Polly, worried how she would pick up her aunt if she actually fell, which could happen any second judging by the way she was listing as she tried to walk across the room, her puffy ankles overflowing her buckled shoes.

"I must admit, I am feeling a little peculiar. It must be the shock."

Polly wondered if she ought to fetch her father's brandy, but decided she had best not offer her aunt the spirit of the devil, even if she did look like she needed it. So Polly grabbed a chair from the kitchen table and manoeuvred it under her aunt, helping her into a sitting position. Madam Grunger nearly overbalanced because Polly was thinking about something else. Something much more important. If someone had been looking for her father's journal, that could only mean one thing. They were looking for the goldicoot.

Chapter 3

As Madam Grunger rested in her room, her curtains closed, Polly could hear her snoring through the door. The constabulary had been summoned to call later that afternoon. If someone else was on the trail of the goldicoot, Polly couldn't risk them getting hold of her father's journal. As a precaution, Polly had hidden it under her mattress but if they tried again, it might not be safe for long.

Polly wondered who the intruder could have been. Her father's quest to find the goldicoot was by no means a secret. The Royal Society of Ornithologists had publicly discredited her father in the Evening Chronicle only six months ago, after her father had published his most controversial paper. "*Goldicoots, Fact not Myth*", was a scientific paper in which her father had laid out what he said were known facts. Polly had kept a copy. She pulled out her scrapbook from her drawer and turned the pages until she found the article she had pasted inside. She skimmed through it until she reached the most exciting bit.

...Amidst the story telling of mythological creatures, there can be found the indisputable fact that there is physical evidence of the goldicoot's existence. A tail feather of real gold was found by the naturalist, Edmund Milner, in 1894, whilst on expedition in the western

*region of the Hibrodean rainforest. There is no known
species that this feather could belong to, except that of the
goldicoot. Up until this discovery, the goldicoot had been
dismissed as a mythical bird, found only in folklore and
the minds of the over curious...*

Polly remembered her father telling her that he himself
had visited Edmund Milner, only to discover that he had died,
in mysterious circumstances, just three months after making
his discovery. The feather had since remained locked in a
glass case in the specimen room of the Natural History
Museum in Wiggington. It was labelled, 'species unknown'.
Edmund Milner's field notes were also stored at the museum
and Polly was sure her father had travelled to read them.

Closing the scrapbook, she listened to hear if her aunt had
awoken and heard Madam Grunger walking along the
corridor, heading for the stairs. Polly needed to know what
had prompted her father to travel to the Hibrodean rainforest.
She knew deep in her heart that he was still there, somewhere,
he must be. Surely if he were indeed dead, she would be able
to feel it and she didn't. And Polly was sure that she wasn't the
only one who believed the goldicoot was real, clearly someone
else did too. Polly wanted to see the feather for herself and
maybe Edmund Milner's field notes could unravel the mystery
of the beast. Polly would travel to Wiggington the very next
day. Madam Grunger, who deplored anything dead or stuffed,
would not want to accompany her into the museum but Polly

knew her aunt couldn't resist shopping, especially for shoes and Wiggington had shoe shops in abundance. Wiggington also had a pawnbroker and her mother's ring had given Polly an idea.

Polly waited until Madam Grunger had reached the bottom of the stairs and started walking along to the kitchen, no doubt waiting for the arrival of the constabulary. Polly had other things on her mind. She ran along the corridor to Madam Grunger's room and silently opened the door. The jewellery box stood on a cabinet. It was a small ebony box, adorned with carved flowers, and had ivory handles. Polly opened the bottom drawer. Alongside the strings of pearls that lay coiled upon the silk turquoise lining was a small leather box. Polly opened it. Inside sat a gold ring, an emerald set in a golden twist, her mother's ring. It had been an engagement ring, given to her by Polly's father and now all that remained of her memory. Pawning it would, Polly hoped, give her enough money to travel by train and then steamship to the Hibrodean rainforest. Polly closed the box and popped it into her pinafore pocket, taking care to do up the button. Her mother would surely want Polly to do everything she could to bring her father home. And father, well, Polly was sure he would understand. As for Madam Grunger, when she found out the ring was missing, Polly would be long gone.

"Polly," Madam Grunger bellowed up the stairs. "Inspector Rington has arrived. He wishes to speak with you."

From the sound of the noises coming from downstairs, the Inspector must have already searched her father's study and was now in the kitchen, no doubt postulating on where the burglar had broken in. Polly ran downstairs and was halted at the bottom by her aunt.

"No need to bother the gentleman with your stupid notions. The burglar was obviously disturbed by something and ran off before taking anything."

"That's most unlikely," said Polly, looking down the corridor to where Inspector Rington stood. He was peering through a magnifying glass at fragments of glass on the kitchen floor, his white peppered moustache trembling as he muttered to himself.

"They were looking for something of father's," said Polly, realising that she too was whispering.

"Ridiculous," whispered Madam Grunger. "They were looking for money or jewellery or both, something easy to trade. What use would they have with dead birds or rotten eggs or the ramblings of a madman for that matter."

"They were hunting for the goldicoot."

"Really!" exclaimed Madam Grunger. "Only someone insane would chase a mythological beast and look at what became of him."

The overpowering scent of Madam Grunger's musk made Polly cough.

The Inspector looked up, catching Polly's eye as she

manoeuvred past Madam Grunger and into the kitchen.

"Miss Gertram, I presume?"

"Yes," said Polly.

The inspector stood waiting, swamped by his wool waistcoat, his bird like figure barely carrying his suit. His fingers were scrawny and white, folds of wrinkled skin hung at his neck like the gizzard of a turkey.

"Can you confirm Miss Gertram, whether anything of yours or your father's has been taken."

"Nothing," said Polly.

"So, nothing at all was stolen? Is that correct Madam Grunger?"

"On the contrary." Madam Grunger joined them in the kitchen. "The boiled ham from the larder is missing."

"Boiled ham you say?" said the Inspector. "Maybe just a housekeeping miscalculation. I don't believe someone would break in to steal boiled ham."

"How would you know," snapped Madam Grunger. "You seem to know very little."

"That, madam, is where you are mistaken." The Inspector slipped his magnifying glass into his pocket and fixed his watery eyes on Madam Grunger. "We know that the burglars broke in through that window." He pointed to the broken window above the sink. "One burglar did not leave this room." Again he pointed, this time to the muddy footprints that stopped by the kitchen door. "The second burglar ransacked the property but left empty handed."

"Two burglars?" said Polly.

"Oh yes and one of them wasn't human."

"Not human?" said Polly.

Madam Grunger sucked her teeth.

"Sightings around the time of the break in report a man with a basu monkey on his shoulder acting suspiciously in your street. The Inspector tapped his nose. "If I'm not mistaken, your burglar left a deposit of monkey poo beside the specimen cabinet in Professor Wimpole Gertram's study."

"How absurd!" exclaimed Madam Grunger, wrinkling up her nose at the mention of poo. "How revolting."

"Quite," said Inspector Rington. "So it leads me to wonder what they were looking for and I don't believe that was boiled ham."

Polly knew very well what they were looking for but why a man with a monkey? She had no intention of telling the Inspector what she believed. That would mean giving him the journal to look at. No, that was best left hidden.

"Did you father have any visitors recently. Maybe I could speak to him?"

"My father..." said Polly.

"Professor Gertram disappeared in the Hibrodean rainforest and is, I am afraid to inform you, presumed dead," said Madam Grunger.

"I see. My condolences, Madam," said Inspector Rington.

"As you mention it, in the last few weeks before Professor Gertram left on his expedition, his brother, Colonel Brisket, made a number of visits."

"I see, thank you," said Inspector Rington. "Well, if there's nothing else I shall leave you in peace, but be assured, I shall be continuing with my enquiries. Good day to you."

The Inspector lifted his hat and bowed. Madam Grunger led him down the corridor and let him out of the front door.

A monkey, thought Polly. There was only one place Polly could think you would find a monkey and that was the city zoo. Polly remembered passing the zoo in the carriage on the way home from the hospital. The zoo was up for sale. How better to restore the zoo's fortune than to have the mythical goldicoot on display for all to see?

Chapter 4

It didn't take much to persuade Madam Grunger to agree to Polly visiting Wiggington the next day. The burglary had, she told Polly, left her feeling decidedly jittery. All her family had struggled with their nerves, she confided, in fact she had resorted to taking a glassful of elderberry tonic that very morning. Polly had recognised the smell at breakfast, it had reminded her of the cough syrup father had once given her. But it was the mention of a shoe sale at Harrisons Department store which had really perked up her aunt and so the visit to Wiggington was arranged for that morning. The carriage would drop Polly at the Natural History Museum and Madam Grunger would meet her at one o'clock at the teashop on the corner of Tunbridge Street, in time to enjoy a spot of lunch. Madam Grunger was rather partial to their fish paste sandwiches and fruit scones.

And so it was that Polly packed her satchel. She wrapped her father's journal in brown paper and tied it up with string. This she then covered with a silk scarf before packing it into the bottom of her satchel. She also added a small green leather notebook, a pencil she had taken from her father's study and a map. Her mother's ring was safely hidden in her pinafore pocket along with a string of pearls, which Polly had added just in case her mother's ring didn't fetch as much as she hoped. Polly couldn't risk packing anything else, so had resolved to buy all the supplies she would need for the journey on her way to the railway station. She didn't want to make Madam Grunger suspicious, after all, she could hardly pack a suitcase could she? Clandestine escapes called for minimal luggage.

Polly thought of the day her father had left for the Hibrodean rainforest. He had carried just his leather backpack with his butterfly net strapped to the side. Upon his head he wore his field hat, khaki in colour, the brim long since worn and frayed around the edges. Polly hoped she wasn't too late. She couldn't forget Mundle's haunted look, the scratches on his shin or the teeth marks on her father's journal. She couldn't bring herself to believe that the beast may have eaten her father.

Polly heard the coachman knock at the door and she hurried downstairs to join her aunt. To alleviate suspicion, Polly had informed her aunt that she intended to study the butterfly collection, which was housed in the Natural History Museum.

"So much more pleasant than birds," said Madam Grunger. "Though I rather dislike the way they stick pins into them. Now, remember, no touching. Dead things carry disease."

Polly reminded her aunt that the collection was housed in glass cases and anyway she intended only to draw them.

"Maybe I should collect you, a little earlier," said Madam Grunger. She stepped into the carriage, stuffing her carpet bag under her seat. "It surely doesn't take three hours to draw butterflies."

"Oh, I want to see the skeleton collection too," said Polly, tucking her satchel beside her, its strap safely around her shoulder.

"Bones, how disgusting," said Madam Grunger, popping a humbug in her mouth. "I'll be glad when your tutor returns from her holiday. I intend to recommend that embroidery takes precedence over studying dead animals. It is far more fitting for a young woman to make samplers."

Polly had no intention of embroidering anything. The mere thought of it made her shudder. She disliked her personal tutor, Miss Grimsure, even more than Madam Grunger. Her father had only agreed to appoint her on the understanding that Polly could spend two days a week with him studying natural sciences and assisting him in his research. Madam Grunger may only have been Wimpole Gertram's cousin, but ever since she had decided to take him under her wing she had become incredibly bossy. Polly's father had never approved of Miss Grimsure but it was the one concession he was prepared to make when Madam Grunger came to stay.

As the carriage pulled away from Thicket Street, Polly wondered if she would ever see her home again. If she made it into the Hibrodean rainforest, she had no idea what she was going to do when she got there. All she had to guide her was her father's journal and a map, which covered the southern tip of the rainforest. The map she really needed was with her father, wherever he was.

Polly watched through the window as the carriage took them along Thicket Street and out onto Blundell Way.

"What good are the constabulary if they send someone like Inspector Rington to a respectable establishment," said Madam Grunger. "A basu monkey in our house, I've never heard anything so ridiculous. He'll be telling me next that it was the monkey who stole my ham. Delusional, that's what he is."

Polly thought Inspector Rington knew very well what may have happened. He was no more delusional that her father was insane. What worried Polly more was what Pruella Trimbleton might try to do next.

The remainder of the journey passed in silence but for the loud sucking noise Madam Grunger made as she consumed half a bag of humbugs. Finally the carriage pulled up outside the large white pillars of the Natural History Museum, steep stone steps leading up to a large set of burgundy painted doors. A stone carving of a lion, posed as if to pounce, stood at the entrance. Polly opened the carriage door and stepped down to the pavement. A spring shower had left a wet sheen across the cobbles and a dampness in the air.

"I'll see you later," said Polly, turning to leave.

"One o'clock sharp," said Madam Grunger. "And no talking to strangers. This place attracts all kinds of undesirables."

Polly waved and watched the carriage pull away, taking her aunt with it. Polly wasn't going to miss Madam Grunger in the least. Polly ran up the stone steps and headed into the museum. She nodded to the doorman in his burgundy suit, gold braids stitched to his shoulders, his hair as white as the stone pillars outside. She headed down a marble corridor, her footsteps echoing around her, past the butterfly room and the collection of stuffed mammals. A multitude of glass eyes seemed to watch her every step. She turned into the ornithological gallery. Now, where was that feather, thought Polly. The gallery housed a large number of glass domed wooden display cases, home to birds of all size and colour. They were stuffed, both in perching and flying poses, either tied to branches or suspended on fine wires, as if flying across the cabinets. Polly would have loved to linger as she had done with her father, but she knew she didn't have much time. She had almost lost hope, when at last she spotted a small wooden display case over the other side of the room in an alcove. Inside lay a collection of feathers, the reed warbler, the whooper bird and there at the very bottom lay a golden feather. Its gold glinted in the light that shone from a high window above. It was just as her father had told her. She read the label, written in beautiful copper plate script were the words, 'species unknown'.

The golden feather hadn't been on display the last time Polly had visited with her father. In fact, it hadn't been taken out of the archives until six months ago. But now Polly stood looking at the tail feather of the goldicoot. It looked exactly like the drawing in her father's journal, the feather he had found in the Hibrodean rainforest. Despite the detailed field notes her father had made in his journal, the same journal that now lay in the bottom of Polly's satchel, the Royal Ornithological Society had dismissed her father's claims. They had denounced her father as a fraud in his absence, lost somewhere in the rainforest, for they said only a fraud would claim to be chasing a myth, no more real than a mermaid or a leprechaun. But the goldicoot was real, Polly knew it was. It had to be. Polly had needed to see the feather for herself before hiking off into the rainforest not knowing what she might encounter. Now she had seen the feather she was more determined than ever. Surely, all the proof that her father needed lay before her but it sat almost unnoticed in the museum, as discredited as her father had become.

Polly really wanted to ask someone about Edmund Milner and his field notes. She started to look around, hoping to see a museum guide but instead she spotted a familiar face. Polly froze. What on earth was he doing there? Had he followed her? Standing outside the ornithological gallery door, his head in a notebook, was Inspector Rington. Polly hid behind a display case which contained a huge stuffed eagle. She peeped out to watch the Inspector who was blocking the exit, the only exit from the gallery, and was clearly intent on entering the gallery at any moment. If Polly hadn't been sure Inspector Rington was on the trail of the goldicoot, she was now. She could think of no other reason why he should be there. Before Polly could think how she was going to get out unseen, the room was shaken by a terrific clanging of a bell.

"Fire!" yelled a guard, now standing in the doorway to the gallery waving his arms in alarm.

"Fire!"shrieked a white haired woman who pushed past Polly to get out.

In the confusion that followed, Polly lost sight of Inspector Rington and found herself carried along by a crowd of people desperate to get outside. Polly was shoved out of the gallery by a man in a musty wool overcoat, who smelled of boiled cabbage.

Polly couldn't see or smell any smoke let alone any flames and this was, after all, her only opportunity. She checked that the corridor to the Ornithological record office was clear then ran down it without looking back, away from the surge of people pushing in the opposite direction. If anyone stopped her she would say that in the confusion she had become lost. Polly found the record office easily enough and its door stood open.

Inside was a row of metal filing cabinets, the contents of their drawers now strewn across the floor. Papers lay in rifled piles, box files lay emptied in a heap. There had been no fire, thought Polly. A burglary more like. Kneeling on the floor Polly rummaged through the papers. She soon found what she was looking for, only someone else had found it first. The buff box file labelled, Edmund Milner, lay empty but for a deposit of what smelt like monkey poo.

Chapter 5

Polly heard footsteps hurrying down the corridor towards the ornithological office where she was standing. Inspector Rington, it had to be, thought Polly. She scanned the room but there was only one small window barricaded behind metal bars. The footsteps in the corridor stopped outside the office door. In the far corner of the office Polly noticed another door, it was open a fraction, letting a shaft of light fall over the mountain of paper that littered the floor. She sprinted across the room opening the door just enough to slip through then closed it silently behind her.

She found herself at the top of a set of stone steps. She ran down them, the tapping of her feet as loud as her heartbeat. At the bottom she stood in a basement with a stone floor that was piled high with wooden storage crates. It was better than no hiding place, thought Polly, but she knew Inspector Rington would soon follow, she could hear him pacing the floor above her. Polly squeezed behind one of the crates and crouched down. Before her feet on the floor she noticed the empty husk of a monkey nut, then another and another. Creeping out from her hiding place she followed the trail and sure enough it led her to an open door through which a damp draft whistled bringing with it the sound of a carriage trundling along the street. Outside, the spring light suddenly dazzling, Polly saw a crowd had gathered by the steps of the museum. To her right, she glimpsed the hurrying figure of a man, a monkey balanced on his shoulder and a wad of papers stuffed under one of his arms. If Polly wasn't mistaken, he was heading in the direction of the city zoo.

Whatever Edmund Milner's field notes may have revealed, Polly was never going to find out. She made her way down Milsom Street, away from the crowds and the museum. A keen wind made her turn up the collar of her coat. She shivered. In front of her the wind whipped up a piece of paper from the pavement and it skittered along the road. What if the thief had dropped it, thought Polly running after it. She could hear Inspector Rington behind her, calling out her name. She had to catch it, she just had to. Racing after the piece of paper, Polly dashed into the road right in front of a large grey dappled horse that was pulling a carriage.

"Watch where you're going!" hollered the driver, his fist raised, as the horse reared up into the air.

The piece of paper swirled past a lamppost and into St Augustine's park beyond. Scooting through the gate Polly lifted her pinafore above her ankles and gave chase, trampling the early daffodils. She was half way across the park when the wind suddenly dropped, letting the piece of paper fall onto the grass.

"Miss Gertram!" called Inspector Rington, huffing and puffing, his feeble skinny legs looking like they might collapse under his weight at any moment.

Polly snatched up the piece of paper before it had a chance to escape. Turning it over she saw that it was actually only half a page of paper and that was badly torn but the words written on it made Polly slump to the ground.

I had it in my grasp, my fingers around its tail feathers and I would have captured it if it wasn't for the most frightful beast you could have imagined. It stood as tall as a man, its two legs as thick as a lion's, with fearful claws. Its head was that of an eagle, its wings so powerful it could have floored a man with a single beat. I was lucky to escape with my life...

The beast, thought Polly.

"Miss Gertram," panted Inspector Rington. "You really shouldn't be sitting in the mud."

He stood over her, his scrawny neck leaning down so he could stare at her. "May I?" He looked like a starving bird begging for food.

Polly held the scrap of paper tightly in her hand and shook her head.

"I believe there is much you haven't told me, Miss Gertram."

Polly didn't reply.

"I'm sure your aunt is unaware of your own detective work. Maybe I should enlighten her at once."

Polly wished Madam Grunger had never called the constabulary. The last thing Polly needed was for her to realise Polly had tricked her.

"Madam Grunger doesn't need to know," said Polly, reluctantly handing over the piece of paper to the Inspector. "I just want to find my father."

Inspector Rington peered through his spectacles at the scrap of paper. His neck gobbled like a turkey as he read the words.

"I was hoping Edmund Milner might have known something that would help," said Polly.

The Inspector thrust the piece of paper back at Polly. "Well, it seems both Edmund Milner and your father have something in common," he said. "Both have been discredited by the Royal Ornithological Society and both are dead."

"My father's not dead," shouted Polly, clambering off the ground and brushing mud off her coat.

"Edmund Milner most definitely is. He died of a fever within months of returning from the Hibrodean rainforest. What makes you think your father is still alive?"

Polly couldn't explain, she just knew deep down inside that somehow her father was still alive and needed her help.

"Miss Gertram, tell me, do you believe the goldicoot exists?"

"If my father says it does, then I believe him," said Polly.

"Hmm," said Inspector Rington. "It would seem that

someone else shares your belief. Two break-ins are no coincidence and I don't think we need to look far to know who the culprit is. Now, I think it's time you were heading back home, Miss Gertram. I suggest you leave the detective work to me. I can assure you the person responsible will be dealt with swiftly. You don't want your aunt to be worried, now do you?"

"No," said Polly. "Of course not. I'm due to meet her for lunch in the corner tea room. I would really appreciate it if you didn't mention this to her. She can be...well, rather alarmist."

"Hmm, well, good day to you, Miss Gertram." The inspector raised his hat and walked away, in the direction of the city zoo.

It must be getting late, thought Polly, and she still had so much to do. She headed down the path back towards the museum and she kept walking until she could no longer see the Inspector in the distance. Was it the same beast, she wondered. The same beast that had attacked Mundle. Polly recalled the claw marks on Mundle's leg, the haunted look in his eyes. She wished he was well enough to travel with her back to the Hibrodean rainforest. Polly tucked the piece of paper into her pinafore pocket along with the ring and string of pearls. She couldn't change her mind now, she would never get another chance. She just hoped she could trust the Inspector not to say anything to Madam Grunger just yet.

Chapter 6

Polly walked down Finkle Street, past the fishmonger and the shoe repairer. If Inspector Rington was off to question Pruella Trimbleton at the city zoo, as Polly was sure he was, it meant it was Pruella who had been behind the break-ins at Polly's house and the Natural History Museum. And that could only mean one thing; the goldicoot did exist. Polly had always believed in her father and she did so now, more than ever. But if Pruella was on the trail of the goldicoot that meant the goldicoot was in danger. Oh what a prize it would be to stuff the mythological golden bird into a cage for all the world to see and what better way to save a zoo? Polly's father would never allow such a thing to happen and nor would Polly. It was unthinkable. Distracted by her thoughts, Polly didn't notice a familiar figure leaving the fishmonger's, with a bundle wrapped in newspaper tied up with string in one hand, and a large carpet bag in the other.

The pawnbroker's stood at the end of a narrow cobbled street. Polly had never been down that street before, Madam Grunger always warned her that the Kings Head public house attracted a very unsavoury bunch and never to venture near it. As Polly walked past it now, a huddle of men bundled through its doors, laughing loudly. Polly had the strange sense that she was being followed but when she turned round there was nobody there, just an old man rearranging leather bound books on a wooden trolley outside a book shop. At the door of the pawnbroker's Polly paused. What if they refused to serve her? She was after all a child but Polly had been rehearsing her story and after taking a deep breath she opened the door, the shop bell clanging as she walked inside.

The shop was crowded with the strangest things: a wooden trunk, lamps both silver and brass, a pair of patent leather boots and a collection of silver candlesticks and picture frames. A particularly large lion's head hung on the wall, its glass eyes looking down at Polly as she approached the shabby shop counter. Behind it stood a man wearing a grimy green cotton apron, and half-moon spectacles balanced on a bulbous nose. Wisps of red hair sprouted from each side of his head. He was examining a gold chain and at first didn't notice Polly. Behind him a clock chimed twelve. A cuckoo sprang out from behind a pair of wooden doors making Polly jump. The shopkeeper looked up. He eyed Polly suspiciously and seemed about to say something when Polly retrieved her mother's ring from her pocket and placed it on the counter.

"Now what do we have here?" said the shopkeeper, picking up the ring in his grubby fingers. "We don't take things that have been thieved," he said, handing the ring back to Polly.

"But it's not stolen," said Polly. "It's my mother's but…"

"Well I reckon your mother should be the one to see me

35

then."

"Will you let me finish?" said Polly, blushing deeper than ever. "She's ill and we have next week's rent to pay and if you could see your way to taking this ring my sisters and I would be so grateful."

The shopkeeper leaned over the counter. The girl standing before him looked anything but poor with her turquoise wool coat and polished leather shoes.

"Please sir, it would be so kind if you could help us, just this once. I'm the eldest and if mother wasn't so ill she would of course have come herself."

Polly waited as the shopkeeper picked up the ring again and peered closely at the emerald, muttering under his breath. The shop bell clanged and Polly turned to see an old man, stooped almost double, hobble into the shop letting in a damp draft that nipped at Polly's ankles. Polly caught a glimpse of a woman outside in the street, her large profile not unlike that of Madam Grunger, only it couldn't be, her aunt never wore a shawl over her head, only common women did that, she had assured Polly. Polly must be seeing things, it was probably her nerves, the feeling of guilt that lay in the bottom of her stomach. Her legs trembled under the pinafore. She felt for the pearls still coiled in her pocket.

"Well now, as a favour, just this once, I can offer you five gold sovereigns but that's far more than this trinket is worth you understand. If I weren't so good hearted you'd be leaving here with nothing."

Five gold sovereigns. That might cover her supplies and the train fare at a push but what about the steamship? It would never be enough. Polly pulled out the string of pearls and let them drop onto the counter.

"We haven't eaten today," said Polly. "If you could be so kind as to..."

The shopkeeper eyed the pearls greedily. They gleamed in the light that shone from the brass lamp beside him.

"Worthless, I'm sure," said the shopkeeper, jabbing at Madam Grunger's finest fresh water pearls.

The old man shuffled towards the counter, a cough rattling in his chest.

"They're my mother's best," lied Polly.

The shop keeper poked them again as if they were cheap junk.

"Two gold sovereigns, that's the best I can do, take it or leave it."

Madam Grunger would be furious. Polly hesitated. The old man now stood so close to Polly his wheezing breath tickled her ear. An unsavoury aroma seeped from his skin as he leaned over to prop himself up on the counter, nearly knocking Polly over.

"Thank you," said Polly, reluctantly pocketing the gold coins as the shopkeeper dropped her aunt's pearls into a wooden box.

"Good day," said the shopkeeper.

Just seven gold sovereigns to get her to the Hibrodean rainforest but there was nothing more to be said. The old man beside her placed a watch onto the counter, the leather strap so worn it was covered in little cracks. Reluctantly Polly added the gold coins to the others in her pocket. As she left the shop the figure of the woman in the shawl was sheltering in a doorway, her head turned away. Rain pelted the cobbles, splashing Polly's feet as she pulled her coat up over her head and ran.

Polly headed out of the main city streets and towards what Madam Grunger would describe as the dirtier side of town, down near the railway sheds and the Smithsonian Emporium. It was a large maroon painted building, set back from the pavement down a covered alleyway, out of the rain. Polly used to love going to the emporium with her father before each of his expeditions. Its cavernous rooms were piled high with everything you could want; from fishing rods to gas lamps, metal flasks and hammocks. It was well away from anywhere Madam Grunger might wish to venture and anyway it was nearing lunchtime and her aunt would be heading to the café by now surely, in time to secure her favourite table in the bay window.

The shop assistant appeared from behind a stack of wooden folding chairs. " Miss Gertram...it is Miss Gertram, isn't it?"

Polly nodded.

"I was so dreadfully sorry to hear your father...about your father. How can I help you today?"

Polly knew her list by heart but already economies would have to be made.

"If you would be so kind there are a few things I would like to buy," said Polly.

Some minutes later, Polly handed over three gold sovereigns in exchange for a small cream canvas tent, very like her father's which was now missing in the rainforest; a pair of leather boots; candles and matches; a metal cooking pot; a pen-knife and lastly a map of the western region of the Hibrodean rainforest.

"They're for a friend of the family," said Polly, not meeting the shop assistant's eye. "Except the boots, they're for me," she said, realising the rather small brown boots were unlikely to fit anyone but a child and what child in their right mind would set off into the Hibrodean rainforest? Looking at her purchases and her rather inadequate satchel, Polly reluctantly handed over a further gold sovereign for a sturdy canvas back pack; after all, she had to carry everything somehow. She pocketed the change of six silver coins and left the emporium, the pack already on her back, the boots tied to the outside by their laces and the tent bag tucked under her arm.

Back on the street, Polly was worried. All that had taken so much longer than she had planned and the train to the port only departed from Wiggington station once day. If she didn't hurry she would miss it. Running along, dodging the last few fat raindrops, Polly heard the bell of a police cart wailing though the streets. It sounded unnervingly close as if it were heading in her direction. Polly ran faster, splashing through puddles as she made her way as quickly as she could to the station. If there was no guard on the train maybe she could skip the fare but through the door to the station Polly could see the train was already waiting, steam billowing out across the platform. A guard, his brass buttons straining across his middle, held open a carriage door, a whistle in his hand, a gold braided cap upon his head.

"All aboard for the coast," he bellowed. "Still time to get a ticket."

At the ticket booth, Polly handed over a gold sovereign in exchange for a green cardboard ticket stamped with the destination, Humbermill Port.

"Come along Miss," called the guard. He put the brass whistle to his lips and blew.

Polly bundled onto the train. The carriage was packed, several passengers still pushing their way down the aisle. Polly heard a strange noise. The chatter of a monkey. Looking ahead of her she saw a monkey sitting on the shoulder of a man who was pushing his way forwards. It was the same pair Polly had seen outside the Natural History Museum and he in turn was being was being pushed forward by a woman with curly black hair piled high upon her head. Pruella Trimbleton. Polly recognised her from the poster outside the city zoo.

The whistle blew one last time and the train doors slammed shut. Polly peered out of an open window, a damp wind on her face, specks of smoke in her eyes. Over the rush of the steam she could hear the bell of the police cart as it screeched to a halt outside the station. Through the smoke she saw Madam Grunger, her face red with sweat, a shawl heaped on the ground beside her carpet bag and a parcel wrapped in newspaper and string. To her horror, Madam Grunger stood staring at her as the train clattered out of the station, shouting words Polly would never hear.

Chapter 7

The train clattered out of the station, away from Wiggington, racing past row after row of rain drenched terraces. Polly felt dizzy.

"Do take a seat, Miss," said the guard. "It's a long journey and you're blocking the corridor."

Polly could only stare at the guard, who held out his hand for her ticket. She really thought she might faint. Pruella was on the train and how did Madam Grunger find out so quickly? Inspector Rington, no doubt. Polly should have realised she couldn't trust him. The guard put his hand on Polly's arm to steady her.

"There's a seat just along here, Miss and they'll be serving tea in the luncheon carriage soon, best get yourself a brew."

Polly thought of her father and the goldicoot. No, she had to be stronger than this, but what if Madam Grunger came after her?

Polly let the guard guide her along the corridor. She struggled with the tent bag which kept getting stuck as the train shuddered along the tracks, making it hard for her to balance.

"Please...where is the first stop?"

"Did you say stop, Miss? This train is non stop to the Humbermill port Miss. Now, how about a seat in here?" The guard stopped outside a compartment.

Polly smiled weakly. "Thank you."

There were two empty seats inside and Polly collapsed into one and dropped her luggage into the other. She wondered whether Pruella and the man with the monkey realised Polly was on board. A large man sat opposite, his moustache so bushy that it looked like an animal curled up on his upper lip. His tweed hat had flaps that covered his ears and tufts of hair escaped his nostrils. He sniffed as if a foul smell had dared enter his compartment and turned away. A frail lady sat beside him, sewing a sampler in a small wooden frame tucked on her lap. Beside her a canvas bag spewed coloured threads. She looked down her thin nose at Polly and smiled."Awful day, isn't it?" she said, lowering her eyes to her stitching.

Polly couldn't agree more. What, in her mind, had seemed a simple enough plan, now seemed like a nightmare from which she couldn't escape. If Pruella Trimbleton was on the train it could only mean she was heading for the steamship which was due to leave port tomorrow and she had Edmund Milner's field notes to guide her. The steamship sailed but once a week and Pruella was going to be on it. Polly shivered. She felt terribly sick all of a sudden. Maybe she should find a cup of tea after all.

The luncheon carriage was crammed but Polly found a seat next to the window opposite a man in a huge wool suit that swamped his small body. He slurped his tea, never once looking in Polly's direction, much to her relief. The tea, sweet and hot, had been just what she needed, though she really shouldn't have spent any more of her money. She was about to get up when she heard a couple talking loudly behind her.

"It's disgusting," the man said. "A monkey on a train. It really shouldn't be allowed, but the guard greeted that pair like they were valued regulars of all things."

"Oh, how horrid," said the woman next to him. "She's the zoo owner, you know. There was a picture of her in yesterday's newspaper. Those poor animals, some of them have starved to death, so they say. It's disgraceful."

"Well, let's hope she's not off to collect any more," said the man, rattling his cup of tea on the saucer.

Polly left her seat and made her way back to her compartment. The swaying of the train was making her sleepy but when she closed her eyes all she could see was the chattering monkey.

*

"Wake up, Miss. We'll be stopping in five minutes."

Polly opened her eyes. For a moment she couldn't remember where she was.

"We can't have you being left on the train," continued the guard.

Polly gathered together her luggage and headed out of the compartment, joining the throng of passengers who lined the

44

corridor as the train shuddered to a stop at the platform. It was getting late. The weak sun of earlier was now suffocated by a damp mist that hung over the platform. Above it rose a stone building, blackened by soot. Polly spun round, watching the passengers spill out of the train and out across the platform but in the crush she could see no sign of Pruella or the man with the monkey. The steamship would depart at first light but that was still hours away and the enormity of what she had embarked upon had only just begun to sink in. Polly's father always stayed overnight in a hotel but Polly knew her gold sovereigns wouldn't stretch to such luxury. She huddled on a bench. She could imagine what Madam Grunger would say; she had always considered Professor Wimpole Gertram's expeditions as madness. What on earth would she be thinking now when she realised Polly was following her father's footsteps, more unprepared than ever in her whole life? With her fellow passengers now whisked away in carriages or walking briskly out towards town, Polly found herself sitting alone, her luggage by her feet. She could spend the night on the station but already the damp was seeping into her bones and she pulled the collar of her coat up around her chin. When she looked up she saw a short, rather shrivelled man, standing over her. He wore a starched blue uniform and a peaked cap and was tapping his foot, tutting under his breath, looking at his fob watch.

"We can't have you sleeping here like some vagrant," he

said. "The next train is not due until tomorrow."

"Oh, I'm not waiting for a train," said Polly. "I'm taking the steamship."

"The steamship you say. Where, may I ask, are your parents?"

"Oh, I'm travelling alone," said Polly. "But I'll be meeting them on the steamship," she added when the station master arched one eyebrow.

"Well, in that case you'll be needing a room for the night. There's a boarding house on Grimsby Street that takes guests, those bound for the steamship. Run along now, the station is closed."

The cobbled streets all looked the same but eventually Polly found Grimsby Street. A row of small red brick terraces climbed a steep hill. Seagulls squawked overhead. The damp air had the unmistakable smell of the sea. Half way up the street, set behind a shabby gate, stood the Half Moon Guest House, though it looked nowhere near as charming as its name. The paint on its sign was peeling and weeds trailed out of a terracotta pot on the top step. Polly pulled the bell and waited. The door was opened by a middle aged woman, her long skirt the colour and texture of a potato sack, her greying hair swept back from a face as creased as old leather.

"Yes," she croaked, peering at Polly in the fading light.

"The station master said you may have a room for the night," said Polly. "I'm catching the steamship in the

46

morning."

"Now why would you be doing that?" said the woman, clearly looking behind Polly at the empty path. "You lost your parents?"

The truth left Polly speechless.

"Well, get yourself inside, I've one room left in the attic."

Polly followed the woman down a dingy hallway and up two flights of wooden steps and she was led into a tiny room at the very top of the house. Polly could almost see her breath, it was so cold.

"That will be three silver guineas," said the woman. "Breakfast is extra."

Polly felt so weak and tired she just nodded and handed over the silver coins before dropping her luggage to the floor. The woman slid the coins into the pocket of her apron and left.

A candle flickered on the small wooden chest that sat beside a single bed, its metal frame and skinny mattress offering little comfort. A thin scratchy blanket was folded at one end and a porcelain chamber pot sat underneath. Polly's teeth chattered. A window, set under the eaves of the roof, looked out across the port. The sun had set and in its place the moon threw a silvery light across the water. Silhouetted against the harbour wall rocked the steamship, the same steamship that had taken her father to the Hibrodean rainforest, where somewhere, she was sure he was waiting. A tear streaked down Polly's cheek.

Chapter 8

19th March, 1897

"Having taken the northern most path into the Hibrodean rainforest, keeping the port behind me, I rather wished I hadn't. Mud swamps hampered my progress. Some so big they could swallow a house. Indeed I watched a margarette monkey being sucked into one and was lucky not to follow..."

By the light of the candle, Polly read her father's journal. She sat propped up in bed, the blanket wrapped around her coat, munching the biscuits she had saved from her tea in the luncheon carriage earlier. She wondered whether she should have paid for breakfast, she dared not break into her camping rations, not just yet.

...I was very glad of my mosquito net as flying scarion beetles came out after dark, feasted upon by swarms of bats...

Polly's eyes drooped and she let the journal fall back onto the bed. Within seconds she was asleep.

Polly woke to the sound of the wind rattling the window so rigorously that she thought it might be ripped out. Outside, the rigging of the boats jangled like percussion instruments, joined by the squall of seagulls riding the wind above them.

An insipid light painted the attic room. Polly crawled out of bed, not sure she'd really slept at all. There came a loud hammering on the door.

"The steamship departs in an hour."

The same message echoed around the guest house and Polly heard doors opening and the creak of the stairs. She packed her father's journal and gathered together her luggage, glad to leave behind the attic room and head out into the salty air.

The street leading to the port was thronged with people, all scuttling, bags in hand to the ticket booth that sat on the quayside. The wooden hut, painted blue like the sea, was occupied by a man with a crop of shiny black hair and a moustache which curled up each side in elaborate twirls. Polly queued up behind the others, her remaining gold sovereigns clenched in her hand inside her pinafore pocket. The steamship, now bathed in a hazy morning light, looked enormous, dwarfing the fishing boats that rocked alongside. Row after row of windows glinted in the sun, the funnel almost as large as a house belched soot into the sky. The ship's gangplank was streaming with passengers and those already boarded walked along the deck, waving to friends gathered below.

"Destination?" said the man in the ticket booth, when Polly reached his window.

"The Hibrodean rainforest," said Polly.

"Really?" said the man in the booth.

Polly heard whispering behind her. She nodded. The man twiddled the ends of his moustache.

"Seat or cabin?"

"This is all I have," said Polly, holding out the last of her money in the palm of her hand.

"A seat down below it is then," said the man, scooping up the coins, leaving behind just two silver guineas. Polly took her ticket but nearly dropped it when she saw the basu monkey half way up the gang plank, its tail curled around the man's neck, the same man who had been with Pruella Trimbleton on the train. She could just make out the figure of Pruella following him. Polly couldn't move, her feet refused to co-operate. She couldn't walk into the rainforest with Pruella, surely she couldn't. What if...

"Do move along," called the man from the ticket booth. "There are no refunds."

"Get out of the way!" cried a rotund man, squeezed into a tight linen jacket. He barged his way past Polly, whacking her knee with his leather case, which bulged against a leather strap wrapped around it.

Maybe she should stay after all. Did she really think she could find her father in a rainforest that spread for hundreds of square miles, full of mud swamps that could swallow her whole and beasts that would surely love to eat her? And what about Pruella and the man with the monkey? What if they caught the goldicoot, what then? Did Polly really think she could save it?

Polly took a step back. She remembered the red face of Madam Grunger, Inspector Rington, the ring and pearls she had pawned. She couldn't help but shudder at the thought of Mundle and the claw marks on his leg, the beast that had nearly killed Edmund Milner. Polly dropped the tent bag by her feet. The steamship let out a mighty belch. Polly was about to turn back when she thought of her father. Nobody else mattered, surely. Her father was out there somewhere. Maybe he too was wounded, like Mundle. He needed help and everyone else had given him up for dead. Polly stooped down, grabbed the tent bag and raced up the gangplank. She was going to find him and prove to the world that the goldicoot was real too.

*

Polly stood on the deck. Passengers bustled past her followed by trolleys laden with cases, pushed by porters in neat white uniforms, a blue pinstripe down the outside of each leg. She had lost sight of the monkey and was rather glad of the crowds. It was then that it occurred to Polly that Pruella had no idea what she looked like. She wasn't in a hurry to find her or her own seat, down in the bowels of the ship, so she joined her fellow passengers who lined the railings of the ship. The gangplank had been lifted. A huge plume of steam joined the clouds in the sky as the steamship pulled away from the harbour wall. Polly heard a high pitched bell. Looking over the side of the ship she could see quite a commotion. A police cart, drawn by a large dappled horse, weaved its way through the crowds, racing up to where the gangplank had been just five minutes earlier.

Inspector Rington! But he was too late, the steamship was already on the move, its engines rumbling as it steamed out of port. Polly could see the man from the ticket booth waving his arms in the air and Madam Grunger's face was redder than ever as she poked the poor man in the chest.

The steamship headed for the Pashmire Ocean, carrying Polly away. She felt like a stowaway, a thief on the run. Oh how angry Madam Grunger looked and she was yet to discover her pearls were missing.

Down in the hull of the steamship, the air was stuffy and foul, the seats packed so very tightly together. Polly sat wedged between an old couple, who munched smelly fish paste sandwiches, and a group of young men who played cards, smoking pipes. The steward had informed Polly that the ship would arrive at Port Natterhorn just after sunrise the next day. There it would be possible to hire a guide, well versed in the dangers of the rainforest, if you had any desire to snatch a glimpse of the animals that lived within. He had made a point of adding that very few passengers were brave enough to take up the offer.

Polly had already spent the last but one silver guinea on

an inadequate lunch of sardines served with boiled potatoes. There would be no guide for her. Instead she intended to follow in the footsteps of her father, avoiding the mud swamps of course and hopefully any other dangers that were lurking in the rainforest, waiting for her.

By late evening Polly felt so sick she clambered up onto deck hoping the sea air might revive her. The swell of the waves made walking difficult. She clung to the railings and looked out across the ocean. She'd asked her father once what it was like to be on ship. He had smiled, describing the beauty of the waves and the vastness of the ocean but Madam Grunger had soon put a stop to that conversation.

"Don't go filling her head with such romantic nonsense," she had snapped, bundling Polly out of the professor's study. "The ocean is a vile place. If a storm doesn't rip your ship apart, you'll think you're dying of sea sickness. You'll never get me on a ship, that's for sure."

The queasiness in Polly's stomach was real enough but she marvelled at the deep emerald green of the ocean, the fins of the whales breaching its surface as they followed in the wake of the ship. The moon rose, touching the waves with a silver shimmer. Salty spray made Polly's face and hair glisten. She pulled her coat around her. A row of benches, damp to the touch, lined the deck and Polly curled up on one, letting the roll of the waves lull her to sleep. There she stayed until the dawn of a new day painted the sky pink above her.

Chapter 9

With the sunrise came panic. Polly sat up. She could see land on the horizon, a dense mass of trees, and the ship was drawing closer. Shivering, she ran along the deck and back to her seat below. The old couple were slumped in their seats snoring. The young men stretched and yawned. Polly gathered up her luggage and made her way back up on deck where a small group was already gathered at the front of the ship. A porter packed cases onto a trolley. A group of men, who looked like hunters, stood with rifles slung over their shoulders. They were huddled deep in conversation. It was just beyond where they stood that Polly noticed Pruella Trimbleton. She stood talking to the man with the basu monkey, only now the monkey ran along the ship's railings, chattering, its tail held high. The monkey screeched as the ship's funnel belched a cloud of black soot into the air. Pruella, her silvering hair piled upon her head, looked older than her picture at the zoo. Her pointed nose jutted out and her paper thin skin was stretched taut over her bony features. She wore khaki trousers, so lose that they fell in ruffles above her ankles. She tugged at a rucksack that was pulled over her shoulder.

"Premble, do keep that monkey under control," she said, stabbing her finger into the arm of her assistant. "Remember what I said, there's no time to haggle today. Time enough for that on our way back and we can't carry anything else."

Premble grunted. He strapped a small wooden cage to the outside of his backpack next to a trowel and lantern.

"And we need that bird alive, do you hear me?"

Polly squeezed behind the hunters so that Premble wouldn't see her. Pruella may not know what Polly looked like but Polly doubted many unaccompanied children disembarked at the Hibrodean rainforest.

The port of Natterhorn looked nothing like a port at all. A cluster of mud huts spilled out of the rainforest, huge layered palm leaves for roofs. A crowd of animal traders had gathered on the wooden jetty. As the ship's gang plank was lowered, more traders joined them, pulling behind them carts laden with cages. Polly hung back, letting the other passengers leave first. Caged birds flapped in a frenzy, monkeys pulled faces behind bamboo bars. Fat fluffy creatures, the size of domestic cats, lashed out with huge claws, growling like bears. Polly followed the porter's trolley, hiding behind its cases which swayed precariously as the trolley ran rather too fast down the gang plank. The porter, sweat dripping down his forehead, chased after it. Premble stopped to peer into a cage and Pruella argued loudly with a man in a huge khaki hat who swung a cage under her nose. The small green lizard sat bunched up inside, flicking out a bright red tongue.

Polly nipped past the porter, sprinting to her right, past a goat weighted down by a pair of rush baskets bulging with bananas and bulbous pink fruit. By the time Pruella had pulled Premble onto the track that led away from the jetty, Polly was already delving into the Hibrodean rainforest. She successfully dodged a guide with hair a slick of black, who yelled to anyone willing to listen.

Out of the glare of the sun, the humidity hit Polly. The canopy of trees was so dense in places that only flecks of light filtered down to the forest floor. The heat soon had Polly stripping off her coat and wishing she'd changed into something cooler. She was thankful for her walking boots. The path, if you could call it that, was studded with stones and fallen branches. Only now did Polly understand what her father had told her. The Hibrodean rainforest really was a paradise. Polly watched a a fat beetle crawl over her boot. She giggled at the thought of what Madam Grunger would say if she could see her now. The air smelt of leaf mould and monkey poo and fresh green leaves and for that brief moment, Polly had never been happier. The air buzzed with insects. Giant butterflies rested on the trunks of trees that were so tall Polly couldn't see the tops of them. Birds flew from tree to tree, flashes of red, blue and green. Nearby a snake hissed.

Polly sat down on a large fallen tree and wiped her forehead with a hanky she had kept stuffed up her sleeve. Madam Grunger had always told her to know where her hanky was at all times and for once she had been right. Polly's father had been right too, the rainforest was the most beautiful place she had ever seen. There was a tree warbler and a whooper bird and just above her, with wings six feet across, glided a mockerjack. Its purple and green feathers glinted in the light that filtered down from a blazing sun high above her. In the blistering heat, Polly sat down under the cool leaves of the bonzo tree and opened her father's journal.

20th March 1897

...Keeping north west, I trekked 5 miles until I reached a plantation of bamboo, though the natives had long since abandoned it. There remained a small rush hut, an excellent camp for the night, though I made easy pickings for the boggle bugs. I wouldn't make that mistake again. But my reward was my first clue...

The last part of the page had what looked like a large bite taken out of it. The following two pages were missing all together. Polly could only guess what that clue might have been.

With her wool coat tied to the back of her backpack and the heavy tent under her arm, Polly walked deeper into the rainforest. She heard a growl behind her. She turned to see a creature, the size of a bear, staring back at her. A mane of fur framed its face, like a stiff chimney-sweep's brush. The creature licked its lips. Polly dropped the tent and ran to the nearest tree, heaving herself up into the highest branch she could reach. She clambered higher until she was almost ten feet off the ground. The creature paced around the base of the tree, shaking its head. Then, most alarmingly of all, it ran straight at the tree, ramming it with muscular shoulders. Bulbous pink fruit rained down on its head. One landed with a splat on the end of the creature's snout. With a roar, the beast turned and lumbered away. With relief, Polly watched it disappear back into the undergrowth, only the rustling of the leaves marking its location.

As Polly sat on the branch, her legs dangling over the side, she remembered what her father had told her. He had been recounting tales of the creatures that lived in the Hibrodean rain forest. Polly had been fascinated by their descriptions. He had shown her a beautifully illustrated book, written by none other than Edmund Milner. The grunzle, a herbivore which ate fruit and berries, had reminded Polly of a huge teddy bear crossed with a lion. Father had told her the most important thing to remember was that they couldn't climb.

Polly climbed higher to get a better view. She could just imagine what Madam Grunger would have had to say about girls climbing trees. From up there, Polly could see the port of Natterhorn on the horizon. The rainforest spread far and wide. She caught a glimpse of a winding ribbon of blue that glinted in the sunlight. A river, and if she wasn't mistaken, the bamboo plantation grew some way along it. I wonder, thought Polly. She was sure that somewhere in his journal, her father had mentioned seeing canoes. He had told her the natives lived in small tribes, deep in the rainforest and that they used the river to navigate the rainforest. It gave Polly an idea. She was was about to clamber back down the tree when she spotted something moving in the distance. Two figures threaded their way through the bubbling mud swamps, the very swamps Polly had taken great care to avoid. She had no desire to run into Pruella or Premble any time soon.

Bundling her tent bag under her arm, Polly headed in the direction of the river. She wondered what Madam Grunger would do. Surely she wouldn't follow her to the rainforest, she'd probably be glad to see the last of Polly but Polly wasn't so sure about Inspector Rington. He seemed rather more intelligent and far too persistent to let a rainforest stand in his way. What she didn't understand was why he seemed so interested in the goldicoot.

Her progress towards the river was much slower than she had hoped and it was getting late. The sun hung low in the sky and she was much hungrier than she cared to admit. Her father had walked five miles in a day but Polly struggled in the heat and had to keep stopping to rest in the shade of the trees. Too tired to go much further, she decided it was time to pitch her tent. Suspiciously, Polly prodded every mound of earth around her chosen site with a sturdy stick. One particularly large mound quivered as if it were alive and sure enough, a stream of bright yellow bugs crawled out of it. Aha, boggle bugs. Polly picked up her tent and moved it to a new patch, far away from the earth mounds.

She'd watched her father pitch his tent many times. In fact, he'd let her use his tent in the garden once, one warm summer night, much to Madam Grunger's horror. It wasn't even past ten o'clock when Madam Grunger bundled Polly out of the tent and marched her back indoors, telling Polly that foxes would eat her in her sleep if she stayed outside any longer.

Once up, the little canvas tent had just enough room inside for Polly and her backpack. She collected a handful of large stones and made a base for a fire. She was collecting sticks when she heard something above her move. Looking up she saw a flash of gold, then another. She watched in amazement . A bird with a plumage of brilliant gold perched on the branch of a wiblo tree. A pair of emerald eyes stared back at Polly for a second then the bird spread its wings and shook the turquoise crest on the top of its head before taking off. Polly watched in awe as the golden bird, just as her father had described, swooped once overhead then flew off so quickly that in a split second it was nowhere to be seen. By her feet, on a tuft of grass, lay a cluster of droppings like bronze marbles. So the goldicoot did exist!

That night, Polly settled down in her tent. The forest was alive with sounds. Bats flitted above her, their shadows dancing across the canvas . Insects chirruped in chorus. Polly wondered where her father could be. Was he thinking about her too? Was he sleeping under the same sky?

Chapter 10

Polly woke to the sound of rain pelting the canvas of her tent. She peered out to see rivulets of water running past. The humidity, temporarily at least, had been replaced with the freshness of morning rain that bounced off the leaves of giant rubber plants. Polly huddled inside the tent, reading her father's journal. She skipped along to the entry of the 25th March 1897.

...I watched the goldicoot circle around me. The most brilliant emerald green eyes watched me keenly. Never before have I seen such a look of intelligence in a bird...it soon became obvious that it was leading me somewhere. Where, I had no idea but its urgency compelled me to follow...

When the rain clouds gave way to an azure blue sky, Polly boiled the water she had caught in her little metal cooking pot which now stood upon a camp fire made of sticks. She wondered where the goldicoot was now. Where could it possibly have led her father? After a meagre breakfast of porridge, which looked and tasted like gruel, Polly packed up her camp and headed towards the river. She'd hardly been walking an hour when she could see it through the trees. Winged insects hovered over its cool surface. A little monkey drank from the water's edge before splashing itself all over.

Polly made herself comfortable on a large smooth stone and waited. If this really were the main route through the rainforest, sooner or later she'd see someone. She wasn't sure how much time had elapsed as she fell asleep in the warmth of the sun. The sound of something scuttling through the water woke her. A small boy, not much older than herself, paddled a canoe, an animal skin stretched over a wooden frame. He wore a cotton tunic and a string of fish lay across his lap. Seeing Polly waving, he guided his canoe over to the bank of the river and hoisted the fish up into the air for her to see. Polly shook her head. She took the map out of her backpack and pointed to where she hoped was the bamboo plantation. The boy shook his head and pushed his canoe away from the bank.

"Please, don't go," called Polly. She reached into her pinafore pocket and retrieved her last silver guinea. It glinted in the sunlight. It was all she had to offer. The boy nodded, snatched the coin and beckoned her to climb aboard.

With her tent precariously balanced on her lap, Polly tried to get comfortable. She wondered if her father had travelled the same stretch of river. The boy paddled steadily. Polly trailed one finger in the murky water. Beneath the surface swam huge scaly fish. Orange lizards sunned themselves along the bank. Overhanging branches cast shadows across the ripples and a heat haze shimmered in the distance making it hard to see where they were going. It surely couldn't be far.

64

Polly felt strangely drawn to the little hut on the plantation
that her father had described. She knew her father had been
there and she needed so much to feel a connection with him.

Before long Polly could see what must be the plantation.
Tall bamboo stalks seemed to stretch for miles, well into the
heart of the rainforest. The boy steered the canoe to the bank
and helped Polly clamber ashore. Then, with a wave, he left
Polly standing at the edge of a crop of trees on a small wooden
landing platform, now rather overgrown. She could see a thin
swirl of smoke up ahead. There was someone there. Surely
Pruella hadn't got there before her? Polly crept quietly
towards the entrance of the plantation. There, in a small
clearing sat Pruella Trimbleton, beside a camp fire outside a
small hut made of rushes. It was just how her father had
described it in his journal. Polly's heart sank. Pruella's face
was covered in angry red blotches and she was scratching all
over.

"Don't just stand there Premble, fetch some water."

Premble was tying a bamboo cage onto the side of a rather
moth-eaten goat that was being far from co-operative. It
butted Premble hard on the legs with its horns.

"Don't go feeding that creature any of our supplies. I told
you not to go catching anything." Pruella was removing her
boots and and socks and scratching her feet. "How come those
beastly bugs haven't half eaten you as well?"

Polly was far more interested in the creature trapped

65

inside the bamboo cage. It was the size of a ferret, though much fatter, with short tufted ears. It had the most beautiful hands, not unlike those of a monkey, and it was picking fleas out of its fur. The cage was so small that the poor thing had no room to turn around and when the goat butted Premble for a second time, the creature squeaked not unlike a guinea pig as its cage rocked violently. Premble reached inside a bag strapped to the other side of the goat and retrieved a metal flask. It was the same man Polly had seen outside the Natural History Museum with Edmund Milner's field notes. And if it were his basu monkey that Polly had seen on the train and the steam ship, then he was the one behind the break in at Polly's house too. There was no sign of his monkey but even without it Polly would have recognised that man anywhere. His tiny round glasses sat on the tip of his nose and strands of greasy hair plastered his forehead. He wore a woollen tank top, despite the heat, which looked like it had shrunk in the wash.

"Oh do hurry up!" called Pruella.

Polly had hoped to find a clue at the little rush hut. Maybe her father had left something behind but now there was no chance of looking and Pruella didn't seem in any hurry to move on. Polly knew that sooner or later their paths would cross but why did Pruella have to be there.

Something moved in the branches above Polly's head and Premble looked up. Then Polly saw it. The basu monkey. It leapt from the end of a branch and climbed a tree creeper down to the ground in the clearing. Premble scooped up the monkey, placed it up on his shoulder and started walking towards the river. Polly darted from behind the tree and crawled into the undergrowth so he wouldn't see her. He walked right past where Polly was hiding, his boots so close she could have touched them. She was about to move when she heard Pruella shouting.

"It's here! Premble, get back here at once. The goldicoot, I can see it!"

Polly poked her head out of her hiding place. She could see Pruella, who was now hopping in one boot, struggling to pull on the other. The shadow of a large bird fell over the clearing. Then Polly saw it too. The goldicoot, so very majestic, its wings outstretched. It circled the clearing, almost as if it were showing off.

"Premble!"

Pruella had abandoned one boot and now ran across the clearing, staring up at the magnificent bird.

Polly moved nearer, trying to keep herself hidden but in her excitement she trod too heavily and a small branch snapped beneath her boot.

Pruella swung round towards the sound. "You!" she cried, catching sight of Polly. "You're the girl from the steamship!"

Polly froze.

The goldicoot swept so low over Pruella's head that she had to duck. In that second Polly squeezed behind a clump of large leaves and squatted down, her heart pounding in her chest. Premble bounded back into the clearing, sweat dripping down his face.

"Look!" cried Pruella.

Again the goldicoot flew across the clearing, even lower still, its feathers a flash of gold in the sunlight. It was almost as if the goldicoot was trying to scare Pruella. An inch lower and it would have touched her head.

"Do something Premble. Catch it!"

Premble ran round in circles, reaching his arms up into the air trying to grab hold of the bird's tail feathers but it was clear to Polly that the bird was in no danger. She couldn't help thinking the goldicoot was just taunting them. Premble and Pruella were so busy trying to catch it they seemed to forget Polly was there at all and she could have just slipped away but Polly couldn't take her eyes off the goldicoot. It was the most beautiful bird Polly had ever seen and highly intelligent with it.

Premble jumped into the air, the bird just within his grasp. The basu monkey chose that moment to come running back into the clearing from the river, chattering loudly. Premble, startled by the noise, misjudged his footing and stumbled. He fell backwards onto the tethered goat, which reared up in fright so suddenly that the bamboo cage on its back became unhitched, tumbling to the ground, breaking the catch. The creature inside slunk out. The goldicoot flew up into a tree and there it sat surveying the chaos.

Pruella stared up at the bird that could surely save her zoo. The goldicoot took that precise moment to relieve itself. A shower of copper droppings fell onto the top of Pruellas's head and tumbled down her hair. Then with an almighty flap of its wings, the bird took to the air and was gone, leaving Pruella shrieking. Premble lay on the ground, his glasses knocked from his nose. The basu monkey clapped hysterically and the furry creature, free at last, scampered into the undergrowth towards Polly.

Chapter 11

The creature sat beside Polly, who knelt on all fours peering through the leaves of the undergrowth into the clearing. She had seen the creature running towards her, maybe it could smell her. Its amber eyes looked straight at her and it seemed so cuddly and harmless that Polly found herself talking to it. Polly had wanted a cat, a white Persian one, but Madam Grunger hated animals.

"No animal that sheds its fur is living in this house," Madam Grunger had said. "There are quite enough creatures here without adding to the menagerie and cats make me sneeze."

But Polly had wanted an animal that she could play with, talk to and although there were birds of all colours and sizes in her father's study, they were all stuffed.

Polly inched closer to the creature that had found a fallen yellow fruit and was delicately peeling away its skin. Polly couldn't stay hidden all day but Pruella and Premble were standing near the rush hut, arguing.

"You let it escape, you complete fool!" screeched Pruella. "And if you don't keep that monkey under control, I will."

"Poor Premble," said Polly. She couldn't help feeling sorry for him. He seemed rather clueless. She was sure waving your arms around in the air wasn't the best way to catch a bird.

The creature turned its head and twitched its ears.

"I'm glad you agree," said Polly. It was a relief after all this time to have someone to talk to, even if it couldn't talk back. And as if to prove her wrong, the creature gave a little squeak. Its fingers glistened with juice.

Pruella started pulling everything out of the little hut; cooking pots, a small rucksack, a lantern and a pile of loose papers.

"Get packed up Premble, we'll have to track it, if you can remember how of course."

Polly remembered the papers. Edmund Milner's field notes; the ones Premble had stolen from the Natural History Museum. She'd only seen a tiny piece, a torn page, but there was more, lots of it.

Premble gathered up the cooking pots and began frantically stuffing them into the backpack. The monkey chattered loudly.

"The girl...Premble, did you see her?"

Pruella had remembered Polly. Polly knew she should run, keep one step ahead of Pruella, but seeing Edmund Milner's field notes had got her thinking. What if he had known something? He'd seen the beast and it could have been the same beast that attacked Mundle, the beast he claimed had attacked her Father. What if Edmund Milner had known something else? Maybe there were more clues. The pages were just there, lying on the ground.

71

Pruella pushed past Premble and headed for the bushes where Polly sat hidden.

"I saw her...in there."

"Who...who did you see?" stuttered Premble.

"A girl, I saw her on the steamship. She was...wait a minute, I've seen her before...she was at the zoo with her father, Professor Gertram!"

"That's not possible," said Premble, thrashing around in the undergrowth. "She's just a child. What would she be doing in the rainforest?"

"Don't be so stupid, Premble. She'd be doing exactly what we are."

Polly had already started crawling and she moved quickly, nearer to the hut and away from where Premble pushed aside the leaves, hunting for her. The furry creature followed Polly, close on her heels, she could feel its fur against her legs.

"Keep quiet," she whispered.

Polly was in striking distance of the hut and Premble was still several feet away. Pruella had moved over to the camp fire and was smothering the flames.

"Keep looking Premble," she called. "Or do I have to do everything myself?"

It was now or never. Polly burst out of the undergrowth, sprinted over to where the sheets of paper lay on the ground and without stopping, grabbed as many as she could and carried on running. She ran behind the rush hut and dived into the bamboo plantation, the furry creature chasing behind her as if it were some kind of game. Too late she realised she'd left her tent near the landing platform but she couldn't go back for it now. Polly daren't look at the clutch of papers in her hand, she could hear Pruella shouting.

"Get after her Premble and get me those papers at once!"

Polly heard Premble following her, crashing through the bamboo.

"I don't know why you're following me," she said to the creature that still ran beside her. "I have no idea where I'm going."

The path through the plantation was too easy to follow so Polly left it and darted to her right, pushing her way through a crop of rubber plants. She found herself back in the depths of the rainforest where the trees grew tall, their foliage so dense it formed a canopy which almost blotted out the sky. A parrot soared overhead. Polly's legs were burning, her sides ached and her chest hurt, she was breathing so fast. She could still hear Premble and he had been joined by Pruella.

"Come back here you thief!"

Who are you calling a thief, thought Polly. There was nothing for it but to hide and Polly knew just where to go. Her father had told her that if you were being pursued by a wild animal in the rainforest you had to get higher, as the most dangerous creatures couldn't climb. That was exactly what Polly intended to do. She spotted a Monso tree, its lowest

73

branches just within her reach. She paused. The furry creature stood by her feet, clearly intending to stay with her. She wondered whether she smelt of fish from the canoe.

"Well, come on then," called Polly. She stuffed the sheets of paper down the front of her pinafore, grabbed hold of a branch and hoisted herself up. She pulled herself higher and higher. The furry creature still sat at the bottom of the tree and now let out a series of squeaks.

"Come on!" called Polly and much to her surprise, the creature ran up the trunk of the tree with the nimbleness of a squirrel. Polly kept climbing until at last she was obscured by the tree's leaves and there she sat trying to catch her breath.

The creature sat just a foot away, washing its ears with its hands, as if the climb had made it dirty.

"If you're going to stay, I'd better give you a name," said Polly. She was so hot, sweat trickled into her eyes. She heaved off her backpack and wedged it in the tree. "I think I'll call you Mussley."

Mussley stopped washing and clapped.

Polly peered through the leaves to the bamboo plantation below her. She could see Premble, leading the way through the undergrowth, his face flushed red. The basu monkey sat on Premble's shoulder, its tail wrapped around his neck. Behind him, Pruella beat a path with a sturdy stick. Her eyes had taken on a frenzied look and her hair, no longer held up by clips, trailed over her shoulders making her look like some kind of deranged witch.

"Come back here!" she cried.

Polly stayed hidden for what seemed like hours and finally the pair disappeared, leaving only a dark scar through the beaten bamboo. Polly wondered where the goldicoot could be. Surely it was long gone and she was no nearer to finding her father either. What had she expected? That she'd find him in the rush hut injured, waiting for her? Maybe she was the one who was deluded. And now without her tent she would have to take her chances outside.

The late evening sun was low in the sky. Mussley had curled up for a nap and made funny sleepy sounds. Polly pulled the pages out from her pinafore and began to leaf through them. They looked like they'd been ripped from a notebook and unlike her father's journal, they bore no dates and had no apparent order. They were in parts just ramblings, dotted with drawings made in ink. Many were smudged as if the book had been closed before the ink had dried.

Polly was tired, almost too tired to read and the light was fading. Then she saw something that made her sit up. The page, torn around the edge, bore the drawing of a little rush hut. It was beautifully drawn. She couldn't believe it. She read the words scrawled around it, the writing in places unreadable.

...never have I spent a scarier night surrounded by bamboo...the golden feather is still warm in my pocket

75

*where I'd plucked it from the goldicoot and I would have
caught it too if it weren't for the...beast...it came...so wild,
so terrifying...flames so close...they could have set the
rush hut alight and me with it...*

So that was why Pruella had made for the bamboo
plantation. Polly felt her blood drain from her face. Her hand
trembled so much, she dropped the piece of paper. What if the
beast had taken her father? What if he really was dead?
Despite Pruella and Premble and the advancing night, Polly
knew she had to go back. She was sure the hut was important.

Chapter 12

Polly climbed back down the tree.

"Mussley, the journey ahead is dangerous. I won't blame you if you decide not to join me."

Mussley looked up at her from the bottom of the tree. He had scampered back down so easily he was now lying down as if he had been waiting so long he needed a nap. He stood up and pricked up his ears.

"Well don't say I didn't warn you," said Polly. She had no idea why the creature had latched onto her but she knew she would be terribly upset if he didn't follow.

In the half light, Polly headed back through the bamboo plantation towards the clearing. Now every sound she heard made her nervous. Insects buzzed in small clouds and she was sure she heard a snake hiss. Mussley ran so far ahead Polly convinced herself he had grown tired of her company. As she neared the clearing she could see the rush hut, though now the sun was setting and shadows closed in around her. A flapping above her, like a flock of small birds, made her jump. She had to duck as a swarm of bats flitted overhead catching the bugs in the air.

Polly stopped to listen. She'd seen no sign of Pruella or Premble and if there really was a beast lurking out there, waiting to eat her, she couldn't hear it though anything could be hidden in the shadows. She was so relieved to see Mussley waiting for her, his head held on one side, his amber eyes brighter than ever in the faded light. It was as if he was saying, what kept you?

When Polly peered into the darkness of the rush hut it was empty but she and Mussley were not alone.

The goat stood, still tethered on a length of rope where Premble had left it. Mussley's bamboo cage lay broken on the ground. Mussley squeaked.

"Of course I'm going to untie it," said Polly, slipping off the loop of rope from around the goat's neck. The goat, somewhat sinister now in the dark, didn't move. It was busy chewing something. The length of rope had been long and the goat had wandered over to the edge of the clearing where the bamboo grew. Sticking out of the goat's mouth was what looked like a piece of netting. Polly took hold of it and pulled it out, much to the goat's annoyance. She searched the ground, although now only a slither of day remained, but her fingers found what she had been looking for. A wooden stick, long and smooth. Her father's butterfly net! What was left of it, the goat had eaten all but a small corner of the netting.

Polly sunk to the ground, holding the fragment of net in her hand. At last she had something that belonged to her father, some sign that he had actually been there where she now sat, under the same moon that cast a silvery light across the clearing. The goat stood up, trotted into the bamboo plantation and disappeared. Polly felt tears trickle down her cheek.

"Where are you?" she called, though there was no one to hear her but Mussley. She'd come so far and all she had found was clasped in the palm of her hand. Mussley crawled up onto her lap and licked her face.

By feel more than anything else, Polly found her lantern and lit it. It was too late to light a fire. She settled down inside the rush hut with Mussley snuggled beside her. The rainforest sounded more alive than ever. She pulled open her backpack, rummaging through her supplies until she found a packet of dried biscuits. She ate half herself and fed the rest to Mussley. She was disappointed, there was no denying it. Had she really believed finding her father would be easy? She'd found the goldicoot but so had Edmund Milner and her father but no one believed them, so why would anyone believe her?

That night Polly slept fitfully, her dreams punctuated with laughter and people pointing at her. "*Only a fool would chase a mythical bird.*"

When Polly woke next morning, a squishy pink fruit sat beside her head. Mussley sat outside in the clearing, devouring another of the same, his fingers expertly separating the lush segments before popping the pieces into his mouth. It was already too hot in the rainforest and the sun was not yet high in the sky.

Polly took the piece of butterfly net and put it between the

pages of her father's journal. She looked beyond the pages
that had been ripped out. The next entry was dated the 24th
March 1897, four days later.

*...what a natural wonder and a blessed relief; a forty foot
high waterfall and a chance to bathe. If only I could have
spoken to the goldicoot, I'm sure it would have
understood me. It had saved my life. Only now do I know
what horror Edmund Milner must have seen. Maybe it
had driven him mad...*

The beast, it had to be the beast. Both had seen it. Polly
took out Edmund Milner's field notes. She turned them over,
looking for what she wasn't sure until she found it. It was a
picture of a cascading waterfall, drawn in the margin of a page
of notes so badly scrawled, Polly struggled to read them.
Edmund Milner described the waterfall but he went on to say
something far more interesting.

*...behind the waterfall I found a set of caves set into the
rock...they looked abandoned though I didn't linger...they
smelt of pure evil...they smelt of the beast...*

As Polly read the words aloud, Mussley let out a high
pitched howl. His fur stood on end along the ridge of his back
like bristles.

"My thoughts exactly," said Polly, stroking Mussley's fur
and wondering if he could really understand what she was
saying. In fact, by the time Polly had finished stroking him he

was making a sound not unlike that of a purr.

"That's another thing you're wrong about, Madam Grunger," said Polly. "Not all wild animals are vicious and full of fleas." Though Polly rather suspected Mussley did have fleas as he scratched behind his ear with his hind leg.

"I know what you're thinking Mussley," said Polly. "We won't be the only ones heading for the waterfall." But there was nothing for it. Polly would have to go, though she wasn't sure what frightened her most, seeing Pruella or finding the beast.

Polly found her map of the Hibrodean rainforest and spread it out on the ground in front of her. On it she found the river and followed its course with her finger. The waterfall was clearly shown and it was in striking distance.

"Time to get moving Mussley."

Polly took one last look at the little rush hut. She couldn't bear to leave behind the handle of her father's butterfly net so she tied it to the side of her backpack. She'd grown tired of lugging her wool coat and she had never liked it anyway so she abandoned it inside the hut. What would Madam Grunger say about that! Then she and Mussley headed back towards the river.

Back at the wooden landing platform, Polly found her tent and tucked it under her arm. The river was empty but for the fish that swam in a giant shoal just beneath the surface. Polly didn't have time to wait for a passing canoe and anyway she hadn't any more money. Pruella and Premble may already have made it to the waterfall and if her father was there somewhere, Polly wanted to be the one to find him. If Pruella was hoping to find the beast, Polly doubted Premble would be able to catch it, let alone get it back to the zoo in Wiggington without being eaten alive. But the beast and the goldicoot were intrinsically linked somehow and Polly doubted that had escaped Pruella's attention.

Chapter 13

Polly had only been walking for ten minutes and already her face boiled red. The weight of her backpack made progress slow. She stopped and heaved it off her back and began to rummage inside.

"There must be something I don't need," she said.

Mussley pulled out a paper bag of dried fruit.

"Go on then, you can have it but I was thinking of something heavier."

Polly untied her shoes from the outside of the pack and tossed them onto the path.

"I always hated those anyway," she laughed. "That's better."

Mussley ran ahead. Now Polly knew why her father always wore his field hat. The sun beat down on her head, even the canopy of trees above offered little shade.

She heard the waterfall before she saw it. A great gushing of water, deep in the rainforest. Mussley ran ahead, leading the way. When at last Polly saw the cascade of water, it was breathtaking. Its spray cooled the air, cutting through the heat of the rain forest. A welcome relief, like the splash of waves on a sun drenched beach. Beyond the waterfall the water ran into a river and from there into a large pool of glistening water. The basu monkey sat drinking, cupping water in its hands.

Polly heard the unmistakable voice of Pruella.

"This isn't some kind of a holiday, Premble."

Polly could see Premble up to his ankles in the pool of water, his cotton trousers rolled up to his knees, the tail of his shirt escaping the tight clutches of his tank top. It was inevitable that Polly and Pruella would meet, after all, they were both seeking the goldicoot but Polly felt more unprepared than ever. She was about to step out from behind the fronds of a large fern when Pruella let out a cry.

"Premble! Get over here!"

Polly saw Pruella. Once again her silvered hair was piled high upon her head. She was clutching a golden feather in her hand, just like the one Polly had seen in the Natural History Museum.

"The goldicoot flew that way!"

Pruella pointed to the waterfall. Behind it ran a wall of rock, stretching out on either side and carved within it were what looked like caves. They were just as Edmund Milner had described them, dark and terribly sinister.

"The goldicoot wouldn't have flown in there," said Premble, walking over to where Pruella stood, his ankles glistening with water.

"How would you know unless you go and look?"

"I'm not going in there," said Premble. "Don't you remember what Milner wrote?"

"There is no beast," laughed Pruella. "More likely a big cat, a jaguar or a munster. In fact, one of those would be just wonderful for the zoo."

Premble look appalled. "The natives mentioned a beast too."

"Naive superstition and an over active imagination," called Pruella. "Milner probably just wanted to keep the goldicoot for himself and how better than to create some scare story."

Polly had read Edmund Milner's description of the beast. She still had the piece of paper that Premble had dropped. She'd stuck it into the back of her father's journal. The beast was no jaguar. The beast was more terrifying than anything Polly could imagine and maybe even now it was prowling through those caves.

Well she couldn't hide for ever and the waterfall was important, it had to be. The pages of Edmund Milner's field notes were safely hidden deep within her pinafore, where no one would dare to look. Polly eased herself out of the undergrowth. Premble clambered over the wet rocks to the wall of caves and Pruella, still holding the golden feather, waited impatiently for him.

Polly headed for the waterfall, the sound of her movements drowned out by the torrent of water. Mussley dived in front of her, nearly tripping her over.

"Careful Mussley."

Pruella heard Polly and spun round.

"You!" she cried. "If you're after the goldicoot I got here first. It's mine and you can hand back those notes you stole, now."

Polly shook her head. Mussley sat, swishing his tail from side to side.

"Stealing animals too, I see."

Pruella strode towards Mussley. Polly was about to protest when a large shadow swept over them. Polly heard something fall to the ground. The goldicoot flew across the front of the waterfall, a flash of gold amongst the spray. Polly was sure the goldicoot had something tied around its neck but she couldn't see what it was.

Mussley squeaked. He held something small and round in his hand and it was made of gold.

"What's that creature found?" cried Pruella.

Mussley burrowed back into the undergrowth.

Pruella went to follow him.

"Leave him alone," shouted Polly. "I didn't steal him, I let him free."

Pruella stared at her.

"It's cruel to trap animals," said Polly.

Pruella put her hands on her hips and laughed. "Cruel, you're calling me cruel."

"You are," said Polly. Hearing Mussley squeak, Polly looked for him between the ferns. What had Mussley found? Whatever it was the goldicoot must have dropped it and she didn't want Pruella to see it. "Zoos are cruel."

"You clearly don't understand zoos at all." Pruella pushed the golden feather into her back pocket. "I'm preserving rare species, allowing the world to see creatures that otherwise they would never see, never know existed. There's nothing cruel in that."

Polly remembered the birds she'd seen with her father at the zoo, in cages so small they couldn't even fly. It wasn't preservation, it was a living death, nothing more.

"At least I don't kill them and stuff them."

"What...what are you saying?"

"Your father enjoys killing birds, now that's what I call cruel."

"But...he doesn't...he..." Polly thought of all the birds under glass domes in her father's study.

"The Natural History Museum relies on people like your father to fill its displays and pull in the public. You don't honestly think he cared about those birds do you?"

Polly felt sick. She had a horrible feeling in her stomach and it wouldn't go away. She recalled what Madam Grunger had said.

"... your father is in no position to criticise... How naive you really are..."

But Polly's father had always assured her that the birds had died a natural death and that mounting them allowed people to see how beautiful they were. Had he been lying?

"Not so smug now, are you." A sly smile crossed Pruella's lips. "Your father, the great ornithologist. Sometimes children see only what they want to see."

Pruella words stung, maybe because they were true. Polly could hear Mussley rustling the undergrowth.

Pruella stepped closer. "Premble. Get over here."

There was no reply.

"Premble!" screeched Pruella.

Premble had disappeared.

Surely not everything Father had told her was a lie?

"You just want to put the goldicoot into a cage." She tried to stop her words from trembling. She couldn't give Pruella the satisfaction of seeing her cry.

"Well, how else can I prove to the world that the goldicoot exists? Edmund Milner had a feather and just look what happened to that. No, a live goldicoot is what I need. No one can argue with that and it will put my zoo back on the map. Everyone will want to come to see it. It's so much better that I let it live rather than stuff it into a glass dome in the Natural History Museum."

"Father wouldn't do that," cried Polly.

"That's exactly what he would have done. He's no better than the rest of the Royal Ornithological Society. They were just jealous that he might do something they couldn't and he was just trying to get back into the fold. Bird murderers, the lot of them."

Polly wouldn't listen any longer. She pushed past Pruella, ran past the pool of water and into the rain forest beyond. She didn't know where she was going, just anywhere away from Pruella.

Polly found herself in a small clearing. Insects buzzed incessantly and sweat trickled down her face. Underfoot the ground was surprisingly wet and slippery. Polly saw something that made her freeze.

On the ground, ripped into shreds, was what looked like the tattered remains of a canvas tent. Polly dropped her own and picked up the piece of tattered canvas. Beneath it lay a khaki field hat, squashed and rather dirty. Her father's hat. But what had happened to his tent? Polly thought of the beast.

Behind her hot mud bubbled and gurgled. The mud swamp! The thick dark mud gave an almighty belch. It bubbled up like gloop in a witch's cauldron. Within the depths, Polly could see something metal swooshing around and it looked horribly familiar. She could only gaze in horror at what looked like a pair of spectacles. The mud swamp belched again and this time the horn rimmed spectacles rose to the surface. Father's spectacles.

Pruella barged through the undergrowth, Mussley tucked firmly under her arm.

"Your father's dead."

For a moment Polly couldn't speak. The words she wanted

89

to say had dried up in her throat. She couldn't take her eyes off her father's spectacles. Had he really been swallowed by a mud swamp? Had the beast attacked him? Oh please...no.

"Get out of there before you follow him," called Pruella.

Mussley squeaked and wriggled furiously.

Surely Polly hadn't come this far only to find her father really was dead after all.

Pruella grasped Mussley round his middle. He struggled to get free, the golden object still clenched between his fingers.

"Make it drop it or I'll toss him in the mud swamp."

Mussley wriggled harder as Pruella tried to prise open his fingers.

Polly lunged for Pruella. As Pruella swung out of reach, her foot slipped and down she fell.

"Premble, where are you!" screeched Pruella. She clung onto Mussley's hind legs as Polly tried to pull him free with his front legs. Mussley twisted round and clamped his teeth into Pruella's hand, so hard it drew blood.

"You little ..." Pruella let go so suddenly she landed face down in the mud. The mud swamp beside her belched. Mussley belted towards the waterfall, closely followed by Polly. As they reached the pool of water Mussley stopped. The basu monkey was chattering hysterically, jumping up and down by the water's edge.

Mussley opened his hand. There lay a small golden fob

watch, only it wasn't a watch like any Polly had ever seen. Where the clock face should have been was a set of dials. She turned it over and on the back was a key hole that only the tiniest of keys would fit. Mussley beckoned Polly to take it.

"Thank you," said Polly, popping the fob into the pocket of her pinafore. If it had belonged to her father, she didn't recognise it. It was such a complex piece of engineering she could only wonder what it was for.

"Oh Mussley," said Polly. " How Madam Grunger is going to gloat when she finds out how foolish I have been."

The sound of flapping wings made Polly look up. The goldicoot flew above her and she had the strangest feeling that in that second the bird had called her name, even though it had made no sound. Now as the bird flew around her one more time, it was as if it was asking her to follow. Polly watched the goldicoot fly behind the waterfall and into one of the caves.

"Mussley, I'm sure it wants me to follow." Polly remembered one of the entries in her father's journal.

... *The goldicoot...it had saved my life...*

"Mussley," cried Polly. "What if the goldicoot saved Father from the mud swamp...he could still be alive."

The goldicoot was not only majestic, it was large. So very large and surely strong enough to carry a man but could it?

A scream rang out. A scream so awful that Polly felt the

hairs on her arm shiver.

"Premble!" Pruella's cries joined the screams and Polly turned to see Puella running towards the waterfall, her face now caked in mud. She ran to one of the caves, the water crashing down so close to her that soon she was drenched in spray.

A blood curdling wail echoed around the rocks and a huge shadow appeared in the entrance to the cave. Polly remembered her father's words.

...Now I know the horror of what Edmund Milner must have seen...

For a split second Polly saw Premble, his face white, his eyes so wide with fear that they looked like they would never close again. Then the shadow engulfed him and with it he disappeared, back into the cave and all Polly could hear was the sound of Premble being dragged and that sound too soon disappeared, leaving behind it an eerie silence.

The beast.

The beast had taken Premble.

Chapter 14

Polly couldn't believe what she'd just seen. So the beast really did exist. Poor Premble. Pruella fell to her knees, her head in her hands. The goldicoot circled overhead. Its magnificent wings glinted in the sunlight. Polly heard a voice inside her head.

"Follow me."

The goldicoot flew towards the entrance to the cave, the very same cave into which the beast had dragged Premble. Mussley sat by Polly's side. The tip of his tail twitched and the fur around his face bristled.

"I think it wants me to follow."

Mussley shook his head and pulled his snout into a snarl.

Had the goldicoot been talking to her? Was that even possible? If it had, why did she only hear the words inside her head? She must have been in shock, it was such a ridiculous idea...but was it any more unlikely than the beast? That was real enough.

Polly heard the echo of wings beating and out of the cave popped the goldicoot, it was flying straight at her.

"Come on."

There were the words again, only this time louder. The goldicoot swooped down, a glint in its emerald eyes, like a bird zooming in on its prey. It was so close, so huge, Polly was frozen to the spot like a rabbit in the sights of a hawk. She caught her breath.

Pruella gasped.

The goldicoot latched its talons into the fur on Mussley's back and snatched him up into the air.

"No!" cried Polly.

Pruella scrambled up off the ground. Polly watched in horror as the goldicoot carried Mussley over to the entrance of the cave.

"I will lead you to your father."

The words thundered through Polly's head and for a split second she was powerless to stop her legs from trembling. She watched the goldicoot carry Mussley into the cave.

"Get away from there!" Pruella tugged at Polly's arm. The mud on Pruella's face looked like sticky face cream and her hair stuck out in matted clumps.

Had the goldicoot really saved Father or was it just a trick? The beast was inside that cave and just look at what it did to Premble. Polly recalled her father's words in his journal.

...the goldicoot saved me...

Polly desperately wanted that to be true but what about the beast? Polly had to believe her father, wasn't that why she was there? Hadn't everything he wrote been true? She pushed past Pruella and ran towards the cave.

"You stupid girl!" screeched Pruella but Polly didn't even look back.

When she reached the mouth of the cave, Polly darted inside. She heard Pruella follow her, her footsteps clattering on the stone floor, but it was so completely dark that Polly couldn't see a thing. She heard the flapping of wings but they seemed a long way off. A small cry rang out. Mussley!

The cave narrowed to a tunnel of rock. Inside the air was cold. Polly's heart thumped. Suddenly exhausted, she stopped. She had no idea where she was. The rock was damp to the touch and the solid rock beneath her feet had turned to shale. She could hear the trickle of water and someone breathing.

"Pruella, is that you?"

Only the echo of Polly's voice replied.

Thud! Thud! Thud!

The ground beneath her feet shook.

The beast. Had it been a trap after all? Polly had no idea how long she stood there. She'd never been afraid of the dark before but this darkness filled her with a fear so great her mouth had become too dry to swallow. What had she done?

"Father, where are you?" Her words were barely audible and tears pricked her eyes. She sank to the ground. That's when she realised she had the backpack over her shoulders; the bag scraped against the rock. Pulling it off she put the pack between her knees. By feel, Polly opened it and rummaged inside. She found her little lantern and after a few frantic minutes managed to light it, though she singed her fingers and now they throbbed. The lantern cast a light down the tunnel, which was carved out of stone. Clusters of bat like creatures hung from crevices in the ceiling above her. Beside her a rivulet of water flowed. There was no sign of Pruella or the goldicoot that had lured her inside. As for the beast, well maybe even now it was waiting for her.

She heard a faint ticking sound. It was coming from her pinafore pocket. She reached into her pocket and withdrew the golden fob. Inside its cover the golden dials spun making a tapping noise and the golden hands quivered. It looked strangely like a compass her father had once shown her but this one had not one but five dials and what use was a compass underground when she had no idea where she was?

She could go back, surely she hadn't travelled so very far but what about Mussley? Polly pulled herself up, strapped the back pack over her shoulders and by the light of the flickering lantern, walked further into the tunnel. The rivulet of water became deeper and soon her feet were getting wet. Up ahead she realised there wasn't just one tunnel but many and as she reached the junction there were three different tunnels she could take. She had no way of knowing which tunnel the goldicoot may have taken or the beast for that matter. Randomly she picked the one on her left and kept going.

She hadn't gone far when she heard a squeak.

"Mussley!"

He sounded so close. Keeping her lantern as still as she could she walked faster hoping the flame didn't blow out. The tunnel twisted and turned and she couldn't see around the bends but the squeaks were getting louder.

"Mussley, where are you?"

Polly's voice echoed around her.

There was a terrific flapping of wings behind her and Polly only just ducked in time as the flock of bats screeched overhead. They had small heads and very large ears and skeletal arms and legs. Great membranes of skin formed wings. The bats' sharp teeth were flashes of white in the darkness. They were hunting. They hurtled down the tunnel, heading towards a dark shadow that lay huddled on the ground.

"No! Mussley, look out!"

Polly set down the lantern and sprinted.

"Get away!" She waved her arms above her head. "Leave him alone!"

A pair of terrified eyes stared back at her from the darkness.

The creatures clawed at Polly's hair, flapping in her face. She swatted them again and again until at last, losing interest, they swept away down the tunnel and out of sight.

Mussley sat hunched, trembling. Polly picked him up and hugged him.

"Use the dials. Line them up and follow the arrows."

Still clutching Mussley under her arm, Polly grabbed the lantern and searched the tunnel but she couldn't see the goldicoot anywhere. She took the fob from her pocket. The dials spun, the arrows all quivering in different directions as she walked. They were just beginning to synchronise when Polly stopped dead. Mussley squirmed and insisted on getting down.

He sniffed what looked like a pile of rags on the ground and pushed the heap over with his nose. Polly knew what it was before she saw the blood stains and the broken spectacles beneath. Premble's tank top. She'd recognise it anywhere.

"Oh Mussley," cried Polly. "What have we done?"

Thud! Thud! Thud!

A hot, acrid smoke drifted into the tunnel and a flame licked the stone. A humongous shadow crept up the wall.

Chapter 15

Polly fled from the shadow, away from the flames and she didn't look back. She darted down the entrance of another adjoining tunnel and kept running until she was out of breath and exhaustion forced her to stop. The flame in her lantern had long since blown out and she sank to the ground. She cradled Mussley. He squeaked and rubbed his head against her hand. Why had she thought it was a good idea to follow the goldicoot into the cave? Had her father done the same? Polly didn't want to think that her father may have ended up like Premble. And where was Pruella? In the maze of tunnels she could be anywhere.

The dials on the fob in Polly's pocket tapped incessantly but she ignored them. Just look where they had led her. It took even longer to light the lantern this time because her hands shook.

"Oh Mussley, we'll never find our way out of here." She stroked his head. "I'm sorry, I shouldn't have let the goldicoot take you. I never thought..." What had she thought, that she could trust a bird? Maybe she should have listened to Pruella after all.

Mussley snuggled down in her lap, the warmth of his body a comfort in the damp of the tunnel. Polly shivered. She didn't know how long she sat there but she was so hungry she rummaged in her back pack and found a packet of biscuits. She fed some to Mussley and ate the rest herself. Well she couldn't stay there but she knew they were hideously lost.

By the light of the lantern, Polly leafed through her father's journal but it had nothing else to tell her. She now knew only too well what must have burnt the last pages. Was that really the end of her father's story?

Polly pulled out the sheaf of Edmund Milner's field notes. Ripped from their journal she had no way of knowing what order they should have been in or whether any pages were missing. A page tumbled out of the pile and into her lap. She picked up the scrap of paper.

...the caves hold many secrets. Men before me have dared to look, their skeletons tell a story I do not wish to know...

Polly thought of the beast and shuddered.

...but they also hide a prize beyond your wildest dreams, a prize beyond value, that is so much more than just the goldicoot...

The bottom of the page had clearly been torn away, ripping in half a sketch made in pen. It was difficult to be sure but what was left looked like the top of an egg sitting in a nest. The nest was represented by scratchy cross hatching. Could it be the goldicoot's nest? Maybe the goldicoot wasn't the last of its kind as her father had always led her to believe.

Mussley nuzzled her pocket.

"Oh all right, but look what good it's done us so far."

Polly retrieved the golden fob and opened the cover. The dials spun and this time all five golden arrows pointed in the same direction, and they were all pointing down the tunnel in which Polly sat. Mussley pricked up his ears.

"No." Polly didn't trust it, not now.

Mussley squirmed and jumped down off her lap and started padding down the tunnel.

"Come back, where are you going?"

Mussley stopped and turned his head to face her. He let out a soft grunt.

"You think we should follow the arrows, don't you? What if the beast is down there?"

Mussley lowered his head and pulled his tail around his body. Somewhere in the distance Polly heard footsteps.

"Pruella, is that you?"

Mussley flicked his tail impatiently. The golden arrows quivered in his direction.

"They will lead you to your father."

The words rang in Polly's head.

"Did you hear that Mussley?"

"He needs your help."

Again Polly heard footsteps and this time they sounded like they were running. Mussley turned his head and listened. The footsteps echoed along the tunnels.

"You can't hear those words, can you Mussley?"

Mussley cocked his head to one side and pawed at the ground as if asking Polly to hurry.

I'm hearing things, thought Polly. That's what it is. This place is playing tricks on me. But what if she was wrong? What if her father really did need her help and the goldicoot really could talk to her? Polly couldn't help thinking that her father too may have been hunting for those secrets.

"All right, Mussley, but if we run into the beast again it'll be your fault."

Mussley squeaked and scampered ahead. Polly had to run to keep up, the light of the lantern already burning low. It cast eerie shadows along the tunnel.

"Slow down Mussley, I can't keep up."

Mussley disappeared around a bend in the tunnel up ahead. She heard him squeal.

A light crept along the ground, shining in the water that flowed along the edge of the tunnel's floor. Then Polly saw him. Mussley sat beside an enormous nest which was intricately woven from twigs and moss. It sat beside a large wooden door and on one side a wooden torch burned, sending flickers of light across the stone walls and onto a large golden egg which nestled in the moss.

Chapter 16

"Mussley, just look at it."

Polly knelt down. The egg looked like solid gold but when she touched it, it was warm and she was sure it trembled slightly as if something was moving inside. So the goldicoot was real and somewhere it had a mate. Even now a new life was waiting to emerge. Polly couldn't help feeling protective. What would Pruella do if she found it?

Though the wooden door was closed, a sliver of orange light glowed through a gap at the bottom. Polly could smell lingering smoke, as if a fire had just gone out in the grate.

"We should get out of here Mussley." The goldicoot and the dials may have sent them this way but something told Polly not to open that door.

Mussley sniffed the air. His fur prickled along the ridge of his back. His eyes grew wide. Someone was stumbling down the tunnel behind Polly's back. Mussley snarled, pulling back his gums to bare his teeth.

Polly spun round.

"Get out of my way!"

Pruella careered towards her, her hair stuck out in spikes, her skin almost bleached white and strangely translucent in the light of the burning torch. Pruella failed to notice the goldicoot's nest but spotted the wooden door instantly. "A way out!" She pushed past Polly and stumbled towards it.

"Careful," called Polly.

Pruella lurched forwards and she looked as though she was going to overbalance. Her eyes flickered with wild delirium. "The beast! I have to get out of here. It's coming for me!"

Just in time Polly managed to shove the nest along, away from Pruella's flailing feet. Her stare went straight through Polly as though Pruella couldn't see her at all, just the demons that had thrown her into such a panic. How long had Pruella roamed the tunnels in complete darkness trying to get out? Polly remembered Mundle. He'd seen the beast. Had he been driven mad in these caves too?

Pruella reached for the handle on the door, a ring of rusty iron.

"There's something behind the door," cried Polly. The orange glow intensified. She could see a line of light now, all around the door frame, and could feel the warmth of a flame behind trying to get through. "Get away from it!"

"You stupid girl, this is the way out. Do you want to be eaten?" Pruella screeched like a wild animal. She barged past Polly. "The beast will eat us all!"

"Don't touch the door!"

A swirl of smoke crawled through the gap at the bottom. Polly dived for Pruella, trying to stop her turning the handle. The golden fob, which had been in Polly's hand, fell to the ground with a clatter.

Hearing the fob fall, Pruella spun round. Waving her arms madly around her, she knocked Polly over. Pruella had seen where the fob lay and she lunged for it, knocking into the nest in her struggled to retrieve it. The golden egg wobbled.

"Careful, you'll break it," cried Polly.

Mussley grabbed hold of Pruella's trouser leg with his teeth but she kicked him away. She plucked the fob from the ground and clenched it in her fist.

Please no, not the fob. "Give it back." What if the fob was the only way to find her father?

"It's mine, you stole it," screeched Pruella. She rammed the fob into her pocket. She was about to open the door when she noticed the nest and the golden egg inside. She reached out her hand to snatch it.

"No!" Polly squeezed between Pruella and the nest. "Leave it alone. It doesn't belong to you. You'll break it."

Pruella shoved Polly out of the way and with a shriek of triumph, grabbed the egg. It was so big it barely fitted in her hand.

"You can't take it."

"Just watch me." Pruella grasped the iron ring on the door and turned it.

The door creaked.

"They'll have to believe me now." She waved the golden egg in the air. "I have proof. Join Premble if you like but I'm out of here."

Pruella pushed open the door.

"No!"

Too late. The flames that lay behind the door burst into the tunnel.

Pruella screamed.

The beast filled the doorway, its muscular legs firmly planted on the ground. Covered in coarse hair they ended in paws not unlike that of a lion, with razor sharp claws that curled out of its fur. But the body of the beast was that of a bird, albeit the most enormous bird Polly could ever imagine. Its wings were folded behind its back and its large head looked remarkably like that of a golden eagle. It opened its huge curved beak.

Mussley whimpered and hugged Polly's ankles. She couldn't move. The beast was so much more terrifying than Edmund Milner's description. Smoke smouldered out of two holes in the top of the beast's beak.

Pruella shook so much that her hand fell open. Polly flew forwards and caught the egg before it smashed on the ground, cradling it in her hands. The beast only had eyes for Pruella. Polly placed the egg back in the nest then pinned herself up against the wall of the tunnel hoping its shadow would hide her.

The beast took a step forward so that now it stood in the tunnel, next to the nest, right in front of Pruella. She froze, like a rabbit caught in the glare of a fox.

"Run." Polly imagined she'd scream if she saw the beast but now her words were barely audible; fear had literally dried them up. She could feel Mussley trembling beside her and instinctively she scooped him up, clutching him to her chest.

The beast took another step.

"Run!" Polly forced out the words.

This time Pruella turned on the spot and ran, back down the tunnel the way she had come. The beast opened its beak and out shot a flame, roaring down the tunnel after her.

For the first time, the beast spotted Polly. She shrank back even further into the shadows, clenching Mussley even tighter, her heart hammering in her ears. The beast was surely going to kill her, just like Premble but a second later the beast looked away. Taking giant strides, it tore down the tunnel in pursuit of Pruella, flames erupting from its beak.

Chapter 17

It was minutes before Polly could no longer hear Pruella's screams echoing through the tunnels. Polly thought of Premble's tattered tank top. Would the beast eat Pruella too? Smoke lingered in the tunnel. At least the egg was safe. Polly sat beside the nest and Mussley curled up in her lap. She thought about Pruella's cruel words. Maybe she'd been telling the truth after all. Would her father really have killed the goldicoot? She thought of all the birds that sat under glass domes in her father's study back home. A tear traced its way down her cheek. If her father had lied, what was she doing here?

"I've been such a fool. Madam Grunger would gloat if she could see me now."

The door stood open. Beyond it the walls glistened, not with water but with fragments of stone which glittered like tiny stars in the light of the torch. Polly remembered what Edmund Milner had written.

...a prize beyond your wildest dreams...

"Let's take a look, Mussley."

Mussley shook his head.

"The beast's gone."

Mussley growled.

"Suit yourself." Polly popped Mussley on the ground and

walked over to the open door. She couldn't see far into the tunnel because it twisted away out of sight but she took a few steps inside. She hadn't imagined it at all. The stone was studded with gems, a seam of crystals and it ran for as far as she could see.

"Come on Mussley, you've got to see this."

Mussley shrank away from the door. The door creaked and the flame beside it flickered. The wooden torch had been bothering Polly for some time. Who could have lit it? Polly remembered how the goldicoot snatched Mussley. Maybe this was a trap? Her father had always told her animals could sense danger but the lure of the crystal was far too great to ignore. Surely taking a little peak would do no harm. She scooped up Mussley.

"I can't leave you here so you'll have to come with me."

As Polly headed back to the door a gust of wind blew through the tunnel, a wind so hot it reminded Polly of the heat of the rainforest. Mussley stopped wriggling and sniffed the air. It smelt of blossom and orchids. Maybe Pruella had been right after all. Maybe this really was the way back into the rainforest.

"Let's go shall we."

Mussley crawled up onto her shoulder and curled his tail around her neck.

A rush of wind whooshed through the door, catching it. Bang! The door slammed shut in front of her. As quickly as the wind had arrived, it vanished. Polly heard the clunk of the lock. The iron ring turned all by itself.

"No!" cried Polly. What if her father was through that door?

Polly rammed against the door with her shoulder but the door wouldn't budge and soon her shoulder throbbed. Behind her came the sound of beating wings. Polly's heart thumped.

She turned to see the goldicoot gliding down the tunnel towards her, the same tunnel down which the beast had chased Pruella. Mussley leapt from Polly's shoulder and scurried to the darkest corner leaving Polly alone to face the goldicoot. The goldicoot and the beast, they had to be connected. Polly had a horrible thought. Did the goldicoot lure prey for the beast?

The goldicoot was flying straight at her. Polly put her hands over her eyes and held her breath.

Nothing happened. Seconds later the sound of the goldicoot's beating wings had gone and the tunnel was quiet but for the whimpering of Mussley. Polly felt so light headed she thought she might faint. Even her toes were trembling. When at last she opened her eyes she was surprised to see the goldicoot standing in its nest above the golden egg.

"I won't hurt you."

"The beast...Pruella...my father..." The words tumbled out of Polly's mouth with no coherent sense at all.

The goldicoot settled down in the nest, her large body filling it completely. Her golden plumage glinted. The turquoise plume on the top of her head looked almost majestic, like a crown. She closed her eyes and Polly wondered if she was asleep.

Polly noticed something around the bird's neck. She'd thought she'd seen something earlier, when the goldicoot was flying across the waterfall. Now Polly could see it was a tiny gold key hanging from a cord tied around the bird's neck. The golden fob...Polly was sure that key would fit the lock.

"I told you to follow the arrows. The fob opened the door for you."

The words in Polly's head were soft and gentle. The goldicoot was a mother with her egg. How could Polly ever have thought the goldicoot meant to harm her?

"I lost the fob," said Polly.

"Then you must find it. Take this key, your father gave it to me for safe keeping, now you must have it. Only by unlocking the fob will you find your father."

"But where is he?"

"You must first unlock this door and follow the tunnel beyond, then the fob will guide you."

"But how will I find him?" This all seemed pretty ridiculous, especially as now Pruella had the fob and even if the beast hadn't eaten her, how would Polly ever find her again?

"You will know when you get there. You must trust me, he's waiting."

Polly couldn't believe she was really talking to a bird, well not even talking really. The bird wasn't making any sound at all but somehow the words were inside Polly's head. How did that work?

"How can I trust you? You sent the beast."

The goldicoot opened her eyes. She turned her head to face Polly. Mussley crept over and sat by Polly's feet.

"The guardian will not hurt you, now take the key."

"The beast ate Premble and it chased Pruella. Some guardian."

Polly carefully removed the cord and hung it round her own neck, tucking the key beneath her blouse.

"The guardian is our protector but she is so very angry, so very sad."

What was that supposed to mean? Why did the goldicoot have to talk in riddles?

"But what if I can't find the fob again?" Polly really didn't relish the thought of having to find Pruella, who was clearly hysterical, and what if the beast had already eaten her? It didn't look like a protector.

"Then there is nothing I can do."

The goldicoot closed her eyes again and this time Polly was convinced the goldicoot really was asleep.

Chapter 18

"Great, now what?"

Polly couldn't believe it. How was she ever going to find Pruella?

Mussley scampered down the tunnel a few feet and sniffed at a pile of broken glass that lay on the ground. Her little lantern had been trampled by the beast. Polly's heart plummeted.

"I'll never find my father now." She hated the idea of trying to find Pruella in the dark.

Mussley squeaked and looked up at the burning wooden torch.

"You know Mussley, that might work, if I don't set fire to something first. It's just as well Madam Grunger can't see me now." Madam Grunger wouldn't even let Polly light a candle without a safety lecture first and she insisted on lighting the lantern in Polly's room herself.

Polly reached up on tiptoes and took hold of the burning torch. The flame warmed her cheeks and holding it out in front of her Polly could see down the tunnel. She turned to say something to the goldicoot but the golden bird had tucked her head under her wing.

The tunnel seemed to go on forever.

"What if we meet the beast, Mussley? Protector indeed.

It's probably already eaten Pruella and now it's waiting for us."

Mussley ran on ahead, his tail out straight behind him and his head low to the ground as if he were stalking something. Eventually they reached a crossroads. Polly stopped and looked at the three tunnels.

"Well Mussley, which will it be?"

Mussley walked round and round, sniffing each in turn, then he pricked up his ears, sniffed the air and darted off down the tunnel on the right. Polly followed.

They very soon encountered more crossroads and each time Polly let Mussley choose. Maybe he was following a scent. The deep growl in Polly's stomach was getting louder and she was about to investigate what was left in her back pack when Mussley let out an excited squeak. Polly's eyes had grown accustomed to the half-light and the dancing shadows but now she saw a shaft of natural light.

"You've found the rainforest, Mussley."

Polly ran to look and sure enough she heard the roar of the waterfall. She could smell the droplets of fresh water in the air.

"Wait for me, Mussley."

With the burning torch in her hand, Polly followed Mussley into the light of the cave. She'd forgotten how much she'd missed fresh air.

"Polly!"

She came face to face with Madam Grunger, only she almost didn't recognise her. Her hair was covered in a blue floral scarf, tied around her head and knotted at the front. Her once respectably long brocade skirt had been torn away above the knees to expose her white bloomers beneath. Sweat trickled down her face which had turned an angry shade of red.

"Get out of there at once!"

"Madam Grunger...how...?"

Mussley curled himself around Polly's ankles.

"Ah, so I was right, Madam Grunger. You see, every clue tells a story."

Inspector Rington was standing beside Madam Grunger and he was holding onto a goat, the same moth-eaten goat that Polly had released at the rush hut in the bamboo plantation. On the goat's back sat the basu monkey. It clapped its hands and chattered hysterically.

"What are you doing here?"

"Surely that much is obvious, even to you," sighed Madam Grunger, flicking a flying bug from her bare arm.

"But how did you find me?"

Polly couldn't quite believe what she was seeing. Maybe it was a mirage, maybe she too was delirious like Pruella.

Inspector Rington tapped the side of his nose. "Clues always lead to the truth eventually," he said. His scrawny neck was bright red. His skinny legs were dwarfed by a pair of voluminous khaki shorts which surely must have been stolen as they were tied around his middle with a piece of string. His boots looked ridiculously large and Polly was sure he could step right out of them. She recognised the backpack strapped to the side of the goat and realised that the Inspector must be wearing Premble's spare clothes. She spotted her own wool coat strapped on top and her shoes were tied to the straps of the backpack. "You've left quite a trail and the natives of the tribe were only too happy to tell me about the young girl they had transported up the river."

"Enough of this nonsense. Get out of there at once and explain yourself and do put that down before you set us all alight."

Polly looked from Madam Grunger to Inspector Rington. This couldn't be happening, not now. "I need to find Pruella...I won't find Father until I do."

"Really!" said Madam Grunger, leaning into the entrance of the cave. "We'll see about that."

"I fear you'll not find your father," said Inspector Rington.

"Well that's where you're wrong." Somehow Polly was no longer intimidated by Madam Grunger. "He's alive, the goldicoot told me and I'm going to find him."

"You foolish child!" exclaimed Madam Grunger. "Don't go believing everything your father tells you."

"The goldicoot's real." Polly felt her anger rising and she pointed into the cave. "Go and see for yourself if you don't believe me."

"The goldicoot may well exist," interrupted Inspector Rington. "But your father only tells the partial truth. I'm afraid there's much about your father you don't understand."

"And what's it got to do with you?"

"Rudeness, Polly!"

Polly so didn't have time for this. She had never liked Inspector Rington. Why had he been snooping around the Natural History Museum? What was he doing here?

"It's got everything to do with me, Polly," said Inspector Rington. "I've been following your father's activities for some time. Stolen rare birds, illegal trading in eggs, need I go on?"

"No! I don't believe it."

Madam Grunger grabbed for Polly's arm. "Don't you go speaking to the Inspector like that, my girl."

Mussley squeaked and lunged for the generous folds in Madam Grunger's ankles.

"Get that thing off of me!"

"If I'm right," continued Inspector Rington, "your father was planning to supply a goldicoot to the Natural History Museum."

"He wouldn't do that," cried Polly. Though she too had her doubts after what Pruella had told her. "Why would he?"

"Money, of course," said Inspector Rington. "The bank are about to take your house, maybe he thought he had no choice. Maybe someone led him astray, who am I to judge? It is my job to discover the truth and of course, your father wasn't working alone."

Surely the inspector couldn't mean Pruella. "But she…"

Thud! Thud! Thud!

The ground shook. A piercing scream rang out.

Madam Grunger's eyes looked like they might pop out and Inspector Rington's face drained of colour.

The beast.

Polly spun round. Pruella, her hair wilder than ever, raced towards the entrance of the cave that led to the waterfall, the beast close behind her. Polly had nowhere to go, Madam Grunger's generous frame was blocking the way and she was swaying dangerously, her mouth open in a silent scream. The basu monkey screeched. The goat reared up, dragging Inspector Rington to the floor.

Polly held the flaming torch out in front of her and the beast stopped in its tracks.

Chapter 19

With a last puff of smoke billowing from its beak, the beast stared at Polly. Pruella crouched on the ground, her arms up around her head. Polly took a step forward. The guardian, if that was truly what it was, surely would have toasted them all by now if it had wanted to. Instead the beast stood watching her.

Polly held the burning torch firmly in front of her and with more confidence than she actually felt, she called out. "I'm here to find my father."

Much to her surprise the beast blinked its eyes, turned and seconds later headed back down the tunnel.

"Pruella." Polly tapped Pruella's shoulder. "I need your help." Those were words Polly never thought she'd utter.

Pruella was about to say something when she spotted Madam Grunger leaning against the entrance to the cave, looking as if she would keel over any moment. Inspector Rington fanned her face with a folded map. The goat tried to eat Madam Grunger's carpet bag which lay beside her feet and the basu monkey ran round in circles screeching.

"Ah, Pruella Trimbleton, I assume," said Inspector Rington but Pruella had already clambered up off the floor.

On seeing her exit from the cave well and truly blocked, Pruella's eyes took on a new look of panic.

"I need the golden fob..." began Polly.

"It's mine, you can't have it. Get away from me."

Pruella darted back into the tunnel.

"Come back," called Polly. "You don't understand. Without that fob I'll never find my father."

"What are you talking about?" exclaimed Madam Grunger. Colour flooded back to her cheeks.

"I don't have time to explain," called Polly. She tucked Mussley under her arm and left Madam Grunger wrestling her carpet bag free from the goat. With the flaming torch held out in front of her, Polly followed Pruella into the tunnel.

"Where do you think you're going?" bellowed Madam Grunger. "I warned your father not to fill your head with fanciful ideas."

"To find my father," called back Polly. She was in so much trouble already she didn't see any point in turning back now. She heard Inspector Rington's voice.

"Madam Grunger, you are going to have to go faster if we're going to catch up."

"You think I'm in any hurry to be killed by a beast? That child will be the death of me."

Polly couldn't help but smile at the thought of Madam Grunger struggling down the tunnel but sure enough behind her Polly could hear their footsteps and the incessant chatter of the basu monkey. As Polly ran she felt the golden key jangle around her neck.

"Mussley, do you hear that?"

Polly had been running for several minutes when she heard a soft wailing and it was coming from up ahead. By the light of the torch Polly recognised the familiar figure of Pruella. She sat with her back to the wall, her knees hugged to her chest. Polly approached her slowly.

"Pruella, I can help you get out of here. You can have this torch if you'll just give me that fob."

Pruella didn't reply so Polly squatted down beside her. In the light of the flame Pruella's eyes looked sunken and her paper thin skin had a deathly pallor.

"The goldicoot told me my father is waiting for me and the fob will lead me to him."

Pruella turned to face her.

"You may have been right about my father after all."

"Of course I was right," snapped Pruella. "But why should I help you?"

Behind them in the distance Polly could hear the others getting closer. She didn't have much time before Madam Grunger tried to interfere.

"I'm sure my father would be grateful if you helped me. He might be able to..."

Pruella's eyes lit up. She straightened her legs. "When I have the goldicoot I could use some... well, a little financial assistance."

Polly remembered what Inspector Rington had said but

telling Pruella that clearly wasn't going to help. She hoped her father had changed his mind about the goldicoot too, hadn't he written himself that the goldicoot had saved his life? Polly could never allow Pruella to put the goldicoot in a cage but if she could persuade Pruella to help, surely Polly's father would know what to do, he always did.

Pruella become excitable. "Me and your father could show the world together, a renowned zoo keeper and a respected ornithologist, his reputation restored. I can see it now. But what makes you think that fob can locate your father?"

She delved into her pocket and retrieved the golden fob which she lay on the palm of her hand.

"The goldicoot gave me this." Polly showed Pruella the golden key she had hidden beneath her blouse. "It fits that fob, the keyhole at the back, but we have to find the wooden door again."

Polly opened the cover of the fob and sure enough beneath it the dials spun and the arrows pointed down the tunnel.

Pruella closed her hand around the fob. "Only if your father agrees."

Polly crossed her fingers behind her back and nodded. She wanted to snatch the fob and run but behind her came voices.

"Polly! Are you there?"

The basu monkey ran towards them, its tail held high. Pruella snatched it up.

"Come here my little thief, come to mummy."

123

Pruella grabbed the burning torch and thrust the fob into Polly's hand. "Lead the way then, before that old bag and the inspector get here. Shame the beast didn't eat them instead of my Premble."

"Madam Grunger's not..."

Pruella was already charging ahead, the basu monkey on her shoulder.

"Polly!" shrieked Madam Grunger.

"Do slow down," panted Inspector Rington.

The goat bleated.

Polly had caused the most horrendous mess, she just hoped her father would know what to do. Pruella pushed Polly out in front.

"Which way?"

"Follow the arrows."

Polly tried to ignore the cries of Madam Grunger and Inspector Rington as they grew ever louder. She led Pruella back to the wooden door but was disappointed to find the nest empty but for the golden egg. As they approached, the wooden door sprung open.

Polly stopped. She touched the key around her neck. The goldicoot had said to go through the door first. Behind her Inspector Rington shouted.

"Now look here, just stop a moment." He struggled to catch his breath.

Pruella had already gone through the door and gasped

when she saw the gemstones in the walls. Polly turned round to see Inspector Rington pulling the goat on a length of rope, holding a lantern aloft. The goat, big though it was, struggled to carry Madam Grunger. She straddled the poor animal, her carpet bag wedged in front of her.

"Just you wait there," she cried, swinging her leg off the goat and stumbling to the ground. "Wait till I find your father. Beasts...tunnels... not to mention bugs that suck you dry...this is no place for a child. I'll..."

Pruella tugged her arm. "Have you seen these?"

Polly wasn't listening. She inserted the tiny key in the keyhole of the fob. At first nothing happened then the ground beneath them creaked and the walls shuddered.

"The beast!" cried Pruella. "You tricked me..."

The ground ahead of them slid open, like a giant hatch, letting in a gush of hot sweet air that ruffled Polly's hair. A golden light lit up her face.

Pruella was struck speechless. Madam Grunger and Inspector Rington crowded round the hatch next to Polly. Mussley squeaked. Beneath them, trees towered into a turquoise sky and goldicoots flew between their branches.

Chapter 20

"Mussley, look."

Before them stood a forest, burgeoning with life. The trees with smooth silver branches were so very tall. Their branches reached out far and wide through tender green leaves. Beside the forest a cool river tumbled through a rocky landscape. The air was alive with a myriad of flying bugs. Beetles and butterflies buzzed and flitted, every colour of the rainbow. A steady breeze washed over Polly's face.

Pruella jumped through the hatch and ran towards the river. Goldicoots glided through the air and perched in the trees. They roosted on giant nests that nestled along the branches. She laughed hysterically, transfixed by the golden birds that swooped overhead.

Madam Grunger sunk to the floor of the tunnel and stuck her legs out through the hatch. "I need to sit down. I would have sworn your father was a deluded old fool."

"You can't sit there, madam, this explains so much." Inspector Rington helped Madam Grunger to her feet and guided her out into the forest.

The goat pushed past Polly and promptly started eating one of the large bushes covered in white blossom, like clusters of stars.

Polly watched the goldicoots in awe. Not only was the

goldicoot real, there was a large colony living beneath the Hibrodean rainforest. Had her father known, was it just another of his secrets? Somewhere her father was close, she could feel it.

"Father!"

A fish leapt out of the river, its eyes like giant sapphires. After the dark of the tunnels and the terror of the beast, it all seemed rather surreal.

"You must hurry."

Polly heard the words of the goldicoot as it swept overhead.

"Go to the river…"

Pushing the fob safely back into her pinafore pocket, Polly started walking, Mussley close on her heels.

"Where do you think you're going?" Madam Grunger blocked Polly's path. "You've done nothing but hurry since we clapped eyes on you. It's about time you did as you were told. I think you've had enough adventure."

It seemed the rainforest had done nothing to mellow Madam Grunger. "Stay where I can see you. I'm sure the Inspector can find your father."

"No madam," interrupted Inspector Rington. "On the contrary, I believe the adventure is just beginning. I for one am still seeking answers. Without Polly here, we'd still be stuck in the rainforest."

Madam Grunger looked like someone who'd just had a door slammed in their face. She sucked her teeth and rummaged in her carpet bag for a paper bag of peppermints. No one had ever stood up to Madam Grunger, not even Polly's father. She'd gone a peculiar shade of purple. She sucked her mint loudly.

"Polly, where did you get that fob? Was it your father's?"

Inspector Rington may have put Madam Grunger in her place but Polly had no intention of telling him about the goldicoot or the fob. She didn't trust him. Why should she? Instead Polly took the opportunity to run ahead. Mussley scampered through the long grass and followed Polly over to the river.

"Well, really!" huffed Madam Grunger. "My sister warned me not to take this position, told me no good would come of it." She crunched her peppermint.

Polly wished Madam Grunger hadn't come to stay. She was allergic to children and animals but Polly couldn't help smiling at Inspector Rington's response.

"Madam, if you hadn't, you wouldn't have seen the most beautiful bird in the world, although I have a feeling this is another world entirely. I do believe the mystery is far from untangled."

Pruella couldn't stop staring at the goldicoots. Polly could hear the gushing of a waterfall and the creak and whirring of what sounded like machinery but the trees grew so densely she couldn't see what was making the noise. The goldicoots weren't alone. The branches were strewn with oval nests, woven from fine thread. They swung in the breeze from long twisted ropes, like hundreds of decorations on a Christmas tree. Each nest had a small opening on one side, large enough to allow a creature to curl up inside.

"Look at those, Mussley. They're just like the nests of the weaver bird but they aren't made of twigs. They're made of gold."

Mussley raced ahead, clearly not listening. He stood at the bottom of a tree, reaching up on his hind legs. He flicked his tail from side to side.

"What have you found, Mussley?"

A white tear shaped face peered round the trunk of the tree followed by a pair of tiny pale blue ears which twitched. The creature looked a little like a monkey. It had a tuft of blue hair at the top of its head and large amber eyes. Polly saw a small paw, only it was more like a small child's hand, its fingers were so delicate. The creature wore a circle of turquoise and amber gemstones around its neck.

"Don't frighten it, Mussley," called Polly. "It won't hurt you."

Just as if to prove her wrong, the creature slapped Mussley on the end of his nose and shot up the trunk of the tree. Mussley was so surprised he squeaked loudly.

The creature was as agile as a monkey but between its

shoulder blades sprouted a pair of pearlescent wings. The creature glared down at Mussley then leapt from the tree. It whizzed through the air, turning somersaults before landing on the side of one of the suspended nests. Then it stuck out a long blue tongue and blew a raspberry. With a shriek of laughter it darted inside the nest and out of sight.

"A pair of those and every kid would flock to my zoo."

Pruella stood behind Polly. The basu monkey sat up on Pruella's shoulder, clapping loudly.

"You can't," said Polly.

"Forgotten our agreement already have you?" hissed Pruella. "Without me you'd still be fodder for the beast."

Inspector Rington wasn't the only one Polly didn't trust. She didn't trust Pruella either and now she was stupidly indebted to her.

"Hurry up and find your father. We have much to discuss."Pruella pushed Polly forwards. "Unless of course, the goldicoot's stopped talking to you," she sneered.

Polly led the way through the trees, Pruella sticking to her side. Polly could hear Madam Grunger and Inspector Rington following but they were far enough behind for Polly to no longer be able to hear what they were saying. Pairs of amber eyes watched their progress and the whir of the machinery grew louder.

"We need to ditch the Inspector and that old goat," hissed Pruella. "And I don't mean the one stripping bushes."

"She's my aunt, well not really. They must have followed me."

"Well keep them out of my way. Shame about Premble, I could have done with his help to cage up these creatures."

The trees petered out and where once they stood now lay piles of silver logs, stacked one upon another. A large wooden structure stood ahead of them, reaching up into the turquoise sky. Cables of gold winched an army of wooden buckets out of a huge scar cut into the ground where once bushes must have grown. A group of creatures, just like the one Mussley had found, nimbly operated the winch and pulley and unhooked baskets full of gem stones and rock. A flock of goldicoots plucked the baskets from the ground with their talons and flew away with them, out beyond the river.

"They're going to make me rich," cried Pruella. "Ingenious little blighters aren't they?"

Polly wasn't listening any longer. A familiar figure sat hunched on a large boulder next to the roar of the river, just feet away from the mine. His white shirt sleeves were rolled up past his elbows, his tweed trousers cut off just below the knees. His once greying hair had been bleached white by the sun.

"Father!" Polly cried.

When he heard Polly's voice and saw her running, faster than she'd ever run before, Professor Wimpole Gertram's face broke into a smile.

Polly flung herself into his arms.

"Well I'll be..."

Polly hugged her father so tightly she never wanted to let him go. She'd found him, she'd really found him.

A voice made her look up.

"What have you been up to behind my back, Professor? Mutiny is it? Your conscience troubling you. We'll soon see about that."

They were joined by Pruella, Inspector Rington and Madam Grunger. Behind her father Polly saw a man's round face, scorched by the sun, his preposterously bushy moustache almost completely obscuring his mouth, each of his eyes looking in different directions.

"Colonel Brisket," said Inspector Rington.

Madam Grunger dropped her carpet bag on the ground. She was so out of breath, her whole chest heaved.

The Colonel grabbed hold of Polly and roughly pulled her out of the father's arms.

"That hurts," cried Polly. "Let go."

"Now look here," said Inspector Rington. "You're in enough trouble, both of you. Let her go at once."

Professor Gertram's face fell.

"I don't think so," The Colonel reached inside his jacket and drew out a small black pistol. "The Professor and I have work to do."

It was Colonel Brisket, Polly's uncle. The very same uncle

that Madam Grunger had written to when her father failed to return from the Hibrodean rainforest. Madam Grunger sucked in her breath and glared at Professor Gertram. Polly's father seemed to wither.

"It seems lying runs in the family."

Chapter 21

"Father, what are you doing?"

Polly had no idea what was going on but she really didn't like the look of Colonel Brisket's pistol or the way he was waving it about. Why was her father just standing there? Professor Gertram lowered his head.

"I thought you were dead," said Polly. "Mundle...well I don't think he'll ever leave hospital. All that was found was your journal."

Her father nodded solemnly.

"Aren't you going to explain?"

The joy of finding her father was beginning to evaporate.

"I believe your father and Colonel Brisket have been working together for some time," interrupted Inspector Rington.

Polly remembered that in the months before her father's last expedition, Colonel Brisket had become a fairly regular visitor, always late in the evening and they sat in her father's study. The Colonel was never invited to join them for supper and it was perfectly obvious that Madam Grunger didn't like him.

"Everyone thought you were dead, every one except me." Polly's voice wavered. "I followed the entries in your journal...and Edmund Milner's field notes too and ..."

"Quite the little explorer, aren't you," mocked Colonel Brisket, leading Polly away from the river, still holding the pistol. He gestured for Inspector Rington and Madam Grunger to walk ahead. Polly had never seen Madam Grunger so angry.

"I warned you Professor, that that was no way to raise a child. She pawned your late wife's ring and my own pearls!"

Polly blushed crimson.

The Colonel snorted then jabbed Madam Grunger in the back. "Get a move on. What the hell are you lot all doing here?"

"I think the question we ought to be asking is what are you doing here?" said Inspector Rington. With his over-sized clothing and burnt scrawny neck he didn't exactly look much like a figure of authority, one who could apprehend a criminal. He walked beside Madam Grunger who dwarfed him in size but when she stumbled he grabbed hold of her elbow to steady her. Her ankles had swollen to twice their usual size and she struggled to carry the carpet bag that she clutched in her other hand.

"Haven't you anything to say, Father?"

Mussley scampered along beside Polly, keeping a close eye on the Colonel who still had hold of Polly's arm.

Pruella and the basu monkey trailed behind them. "Colonel, I..."

"Shut up Pruella. It's pretty obvious what you're doing

here and you can keep your hands off my workers."

"Have you forgotten our little relationship, Colonel..." blustered Pruella.

"I may have supplied your zoo with specimens but this discovery is not for sale."

Polly's father had still not spoken.

"Come now, Professor, do I have to do everything?" snapped Colonel Brisket.

"I'm sorry, Polly," her father muttered.

"What the Professor is trying to say is that we are extracting gold and precious gem stones. There are treasures here beyond your wildest dreams and Edmund Milner led us straight here. It was just as well that no one believed the words of a delirious lunatic and luckily for us he died very quickly. Thanks to my brother's inspired decision to remove all the pages relating to this world, we have this place all to ourselves."

So that explained why Edmund Milner's field notes looked like they'd been torn from a journal.

"So much more lucrative than just selling a goldicoot to the Natural History Museum. But then, I always was far more ambitious than my younger brother."

"So you really were going to kill the goldicoot," cried Polly. "But I thought...you always said..."

"Oh the naivety of children. It's just a shame, Professor, that you didn't listen to Madam Grunger's advice to teach

Polly needlepoint instead of how to pitch a tent."

Madam Grunger grumbled under her breath.

Polly looked at the devastation around her. The land had been ripped apart. So many trees, once home for the goldicoots, lay as piles of discarded timber. "Why would the goldicoots help you and the..." Polly pointed to the winged creatures that worked alongside the goldicoots.

"It's surprising how co-operative the goldicoots and the loopins became once they were given enough incentive," laughed Colonel Brisket.

Polly shuddered at the sound of that. She desperately wanted to talk to her father but the Colonel marched her along at a brisk pace and her father dropped back, behind them. It really wasn't the reunion she had hoped for back in her tent in the rainforest. They were heading out of the trees. The river curved away from them.

"Just look at that," exclaimed Pruella.

A small wooden canoe paddled along the river, one loopin pulling each oar through the water. Another loopin threw a fishing line over the side. Seconds later the loopin pulled it back in and a fish flapped on the end of the line.

"Remarkable!"

"The loopins are the most inventive creatures," said Colonel Brisket.

The crash of the waterfall Polly had heard earlier was now a roar in the distance.

"But fishing is nothing," boasted the Colonel. "Loopins can craft anything out of gold."

"You won't get away with treating a member of her Majesty's constabulary like a prisoner," called out Inspector Rington.

Madam Grunger had stopped to rest on a large rock. She dabbed her face with a polka dot handkerchief. "I simply can't walk another step," she panted. "This is outrageous!"

Seeing Madam Grunger, usually so cool and composed, now looking redder than a post box, Polly couldn't help but feel sorry for her, something she didn't think could ever have been possible. The sun beat down relentlessly from a cloudless sky. Colonel Brisket wore a hard khaki field hat, khaki breeches and a jacket, stained with large sweat patches, belted tightly around his squat barrel shaped middle. He looked like a puffed up Major in charge of an army, in denial of the heat.

"You're about to see for yourselves the reason why soon I will be the richest man in the entire world. But unfortunately for you, you will never get to tell anyone."

"You can't..." Polly's father grabbed his brother's arm.

"You should have thought about that before you contrived to have this lot gatecrash my operation. Don't think I won't shoot my own brother. Sentimentality never made anyone rich."

"I won't let you hurt her."

Colonel Brisket spun round and pointed his pistol into his brother's chest. The Colonel's moustache quivered.

"You, brother, may be the professor but you lack imagination and vision and for that reason you will soon no longer be of any further use to me."

"Let Polly go, she's just a child!"

At least her father was actually doing something but his gesture was met with a pistol aimed even higher.

"Unfortunately for you that is clearly not true. No child could find her way alone to the Hibrodean rainforest, navigate a tunnel system and survive a beast. So either, that child has had help or she's no ordinary child." The Colonel stared at the others.

Polly rubbed her arm, which now throbbed. She scooped up Mussley and he nuzzled her face and beat his tail. The Colonel clearly didn't know about the golden fob or that Polly had been guided by the goldicoot and she wanted to keep it that way.

Pruella let out a shriek of excitement and started running.

Colonel Brisket twisted round. "Come back here!" Pruella ignored him and kept running towards the waterfall that Polly could now see in the distance.

It wasn't water that crashed down into the pool beneath, it was molten gold. It glinted in the sun as it fell in a continuous sheet. The pool, surrounded by giant boulders, looked like a smelting pot.

Chapter 22

A loopin ladled bubbling liquid into a bucket of water to cool. Then it picked up the bucket and flew with it, away from the golden waterfall and into the cover of a crop of trees.

"Liquid gold!" cried Pruella, reaching out her hand to touch it.

"Get away from it!" bellowed Colonel Brisket. "It turns everything it touches into solid gold, look." He grabbed a stick from the ground and dipped it into the golden pool and sure enough when he removed the stick half of it had turned to gold.

Pruella's eyes sparkled. "What are those loopins doing?"

"Don't go getting any ideas Pruella." The Colonel pointed his pistol at her and gestured for her to move away from the waterfall. "They're ingenious little creatures. It seems they can craft anything from gold. You may as well see for yourself what the Professor here has helped me to discover."

"It was Edmund Milner's discovery."

Her father stood beside Polly now. "His field notes described the waterfall and the loopins. He'd even slipped a gold leaf between the pages." Polly's father took a golden leaf from his shirt pocket.

"Why did no-one believe him?" said Polly.

Madam Grunger sat down ungainly on her carpet bag,

revealing even more of her huge white bloomers. "And I thought your father had crazy ideas."

Inspector Rington pushed his way forward. "Edmund Milner was by all accounts delirious when he returned from the Hibrodean rainforest. It was his sister who presented his work to the Royal Ornithological Society."

"It was a remarkable story but simply unbelievable," added Polly's father. " Of course they denounced him as a fraud."

"But what about the goldicoot feather?" said Polly.

"It was indisputably a feather, even the Natural History Museum could see that," said her father. "But Edmund Milner was in no position to prove its origin by this point. In fact the fever would see him dead in less than two months. It was his sister who asked the Natural History Museum to keep his field notes but the most they were prepared to do was display the goldicoot feather as 'species unknown'.

"All the better for us," bellowed the Colonel. "Lead the way to the loopins, Professor, I was heading there myself anyway."

The pistol still in his hand, Colonel Brisket pushed Polly's father ahead of them. Pruella followed, the basu monkey sitting up on her shoulder, his tail wrapped around her neck. Polly walked with Madam Grunger and Inspector Rington and Mussley scampered along at her heel. Her father led them through a dense forest and after they'd been walking for several minutes Polly saw the most astonishing sight. A ginormous tree, with a trunk as wide as a house, with long twisted branches that wove a thick canopy above them. A wooden door on golden hinges stood open in the base of its trunk.

Polly's father ducked inside and Polly and the others followed. The air was stale and hot and smelt of leaf mould. It took a few seconds for Polly's eyes to adjust. The tree had been carved to create an amazing structure; floors spiralled around the inside, each housing workrooms where loopins crouched on small wooden benches. There the creatures chiselled away at lumps of gold, heating it in small furnaces and hammering the hot molten metal into shape, their fingers working with skilful precision. Windows had been cut into the tree trunk to allow light to filter in and small lanterns were strung around, each containing a tiny glow worm. It was the most bizarre sight Polly had ever seen.

Teetering in a pile in the very centre of the hollow tree was a tower of golden objects: boxes, lanterns, tightly woven baskets, goblets, buckets and orbs. Scattered between them lay necklaces and bracelets encrusted with brilliant emeralds and radiant rubies. The horde of golden treasure made Pruella shriek out loud. It looked like something out of a fairytale and Polly wouldn't have been at all surprised to see a dragon guarding it.

"Unbelievable," said Inspector Rington. "And to think I believed this was all about a bird."

"Oh, but it is." The Colonel plucked up a golden orb and lay it on the palm of his hand. "You see drinking from the waterfall is what makes the goldicoots golden. Unlike any of us, they don't turn to solid gold. Quite the contrary, it is their life force, what runs through their veins."

Madam Grunger stooped down and picked up a necklace that was studded with emeralds; it was small enough to fit around a loopin's neck.

The Colonel snatched it from her. "They have an eye for finery. Just wait until I show the world."

"But you can't," cried Polly. "It belongs to the goldicoots and the loopins..."

"That's where you're wrong," roared the Colonel.

Just feet away a loopin sat affixing a cluster of rubies to a golden crown.

The fob! The loopins must have made the golden fob that lay hidden in her pinafore pocket. She remembered the Colonel's words, "*mutiny.*" Had her father led her here? Had the goldicoots and loopins helped him? She wished she could talk to her father in private but the Colonel was deliberately keeping them apart; that in itself was suspicious.

The Colonel removed his field hat, picked up the crown and tried it on for size.

"Excellent," he cried. "I must congratulate my brother on his discovery. He always was terribly good at finding new species."

143

The Colonel looked at Polly's father and she was surprised to see the horror in his eyes.

"It's a pity you can't take up your place again in the bosom of the Royal Ornithological Society," continued the Colonel. " I lied I'm afraid, but you've probably guessed that."

The Colonel looked ridiculous and he was oblivious of how each of his words stung her father but Polly saw him wince at every revelation.

"I had intended to keep my word and share all this with you, brother. After all, it's your discovery, your detective work which led us to Edmund Milner's field notes in the first place. As you rightly argued, it was a prize worth pursuing. And as you promised, my investment in your expeditions have rewarded me well."

Polly couldn't, didn't want to believe what she was hearing. She didn't want to listen any more. Madam Grunger and Inspector Rington, even Pruella, knew her father better than she did, it seemed. She couldn't even look at her father, she felt sick.

"As Inspector Rington here has already guessed, my partnership with your father, Polly, has over the years boosted the collection of the Natural History Museum and filled both our pockets. But alas, there can only be one king and that will be me."

Polly's legs turned to water and she thought she might actually faint. Madam Grunger put her arm around Polly's shoulders and she felt herself sagging against her. But it wasn't long before shock flared into anger.

"You lied to me!" Polly glared at her father. "You killed those birds, all of them, didn't you? And you were going to kill the goldicoot too."

"Polly, you have to listen, let me explain."

Polly's father reached out for her but she pushed him away.

"I believed in you. I thought…how could you do such a thing?" Polly's voice grew louder as her words tumbled out. She could see the effect on her father, the guilt in every line on his face.

"You wrote in your journal that the goldicoot saved you…and now you're stealing from them, destroying where they live and for what?"

"For money of course," interrupted the Colonel. "Far more reliable than misplaced love and loyalty."

"It was a mistake, please Polly, listen to me. When I realised what he was planning to do…well it was too late."

Polly turned her back on her father. She wasn't going to give him the satisfaction of seeing her cry.

"Polly, when I saw you, I almost didn't believe my eyes. I never really believed you'd come, that you would actually find me and…"

"Well I wish I hadn't!" Polly buried her face into Madam Grunger's ample chest and even though Madam Grunger

145

detested human contact, she hugged Polly tightly.

Chapter 23

"The professor here has work to do. I'm sure he'll see how necessary it is once you are comfortable."

"What are you going to do?" Polly's father stood up to his brother but his voice betrayed his fear. Polly had never seen her father seem so small, so ineffectual as he did now, almost begging and to a man who only weeks earlier had sat in Polly's home, an uncle, nothing more than a curious man she barely knew.

"What's good enough for the queen must surely be good enough for your intrepid explorers here."

The Colonel removed his crown, tucked it under his arm and ushered them all back out of the tree, the pistol now prodded firmly into her father's lower back, until they stood in the glare of the midday sun.

"I'm sure there's room for all of you, well, maybe not for that."

The Colonel kicked out at Mussley who cowered by Polly's ankle. Mussley snarled, baring his sharp white teeth.

"Don't touch him." Polly snatched up Mussley and squeezed him tightly.

"Very well, have it your way but as for that…" He reached out to grab hold of the basu monkey which sat on Pruella's shoulder. "He's going back to where he belongs."

Just as the Colonel's fat fingers grabbed for the monkey's fur, the monkey lunged at him, sinking his teeth into the first available bit of flesh.

"You filthy beast!" cursed the Colonel, shaking his hand now dripping with blood. "I'll..."

The basu monkey shrieked then leapt from Pruella's shoulder and raced across to the nearest tree which it scaled in seconds to the very top. There the monkey sat, clapping hysterically. The Colonel's face turned a hideous shade of purple and for a few seconds Polly was sure he might actually explode with rage. She held Mussley even tighter. Her father's eyes pleaded with her but Polly blanked him.

With his hand wrapped in a bloodied handkerchief, the Colonel gestured for the others to follow. Polly heard Inspector Rington whisper to Madam Grunger. Polly's heart pounded as they were led deeper into the cover of the trees, the only comfort Mussley's heartbeat so close to her own and the feel of his soft fur against her skin.

Though they hadn't walked far Polly felt exhausted. Mussley was far heavier than she'd expected but she couldn't let him out of her sight. They'd walked through a forest of tall sleek trees and now stood in a clearing of silvery grass and bushes so thick with white blossom it could almost be mistaken for snow but for the beautiful fragrance that perfumed the breeze which was as gentle as a spring morning. But the illusion of serenity was broken by a giant golden

148

palace which rose up like a temple before them.

What must once have been an enchanting palace was now a surreal prison. Inside its beautifully engineered arches, domed roofs and intricately crafted corridors and balconies, swung at its heart a huge cage. Polly had wondered what the Colonel had meant by a queen but now she could see her, squeezed into a cage far too small to house her. The goldicoot, twice the size of any other Polly had seen, slumped on a wooden perch, her turquoise plume squashed upon her head, her tail feathers protruding through the bars. A ring of emeralds sparkled around her neck, the same colour as her eyes only these were dull in comparison and looked out into space, seemingly unaware of all the faces staring at her.

Polly caught her breath. The cage was suspended above a large room open to the forest at the front but beside the cage, nailed into the wall were three goldicoots, strung up by their feet, all life long since gone, their eyelids closed forever.

"It didn't take much for the goldicoots to realise they should co-operate. They're fiercely loyal, some too much so."

Polly spun round to confront her father. Without his glasses he looked old and so very weary. His hair, no longer slicked back away from his face, had become tufts upon his head and white stubble grew across his chin.

"Did you do this?" Polly struggled to keep her voice from wavering.

"I didn't meant to let it happen, I…"

"Why am I not surprised?" cut in Madam Grunger, dropping her carpet bag to the ground.

"It wasn't my idea, I promise. I would never..."

Madam Grunger tutted under her breath.

"What a waste," said Pruella, wiping her face with the back of her sleeve. Her hair had escaped the confines of her bun and trailed around her shoulders.

Inspector Rington nodded sagely. "A crying shame, all of it."

"Needs must," said the Colonel opening wide a large door which revealed a staircase of solid gold steps. "Shall we?"

"I always thought the Colonel was a bad lot," sneered Madam Grunger, grabbing hold of her carpet bag again and shuffling forwards, sweat giving her over-inflated face the look of a boiled ham. "Ever since I found him thieving my crystallised ginger. No one steals from my kitchen."

Pruella laughed. Inspector Rington gave her a knowing look. "Always after something that didn't belong to him."

Polly remembered the break-in and their dinner missing from the larder.

"Aren't they the prizes always worth having?" snapped the Colonel. "Welcome to my headquarters and soon to be my home. Follow me."

Polly's father reluctantly led the way. Polly helped Madam Grunger who stumbled on the steps, struggling to keep up with the others.

"Really! He's insufferable, but then bullies usually are."

Polly felt rather sorry for Madam Grunger. Without her fearsomely formal clothes she was beginning to look like an old woman. When Madam Grunger thanked Polly and touched her arm Polly wondered why she'd ever been afraid of her.

At the top of the steps they stood on a balcony which overlooked the goldicoot queen. The Colonel clapped his hands and a band of loopins swung down from an upper balcony, dragging behind them a large metal cage. Polly watched in horror as they hoisted it with ropes so that it hung just above the floor. He flung open the door. The floor of the cage was made from roughly sawn wood and the bars of the cage were so close together Polly doubted she would even fit a hand through them.

One by one Polly and the others were forced to squeeze inside and the door was slammed closed behind them.

"Back to the mine shaft unless you want to join them," bellowed the Colonel, pushing Polly's father away. She watched her father leave. Naively she had imagined that when at last she found her father they would head back home together to a magnificent welcome. She could hardly believe that instead she was swinging in a cage with Pruella squashed on one side and Madam Grunger and Inspector Rington on the other. There was so little room that Polly had to crouch on top of Madam Grunger's carpet bag with Mussley curled up around her shoulders. Polly caught a glimpse of a small face hiding behind an archway. It was the basu monkey and it was most definitely up to something.

Chapter 24

Several minutes of silence followed but for Mussley scratching the floor of the cage as if he could dig his way out.

"Well I never," said Inspector Rington. "I don't think I've ever been so wrong about a case."

Madam Grunger sucked on a peppermint, beads of sweat trickling down her neck. "I can't abide the smell in here, it's stifling," she mumbled mid-crunch. "I wish I'd packed my smelling salts. I rather fear I may pass out at any moment."

"Don't go falling on me," snapped Pruella, struggling to pull herself up. She too had spotted the basu monkey and called out to where he sat watching them from his hiding place. "Come here my lovely," she cooed.

Mussley squeaked.

Polly struggled to accept what her father had clearly become without her even suspecting it. To think she'd risked her life and for what? A criminal. She wanted to cry but Madam Grunger forbade any such behaviour unbecoming to a lady, so Polly stroked Mussley instead, tears threatening to fall.

"We need an escape plan," mused Inspector Rington, rummaging in his pocket for his notebook and pencil.

The basu monkey scampered along the balcony and climbed up the side of the cage. He poked his hands through the bars. That's when Polly had an idea. The basu monkey had surely been trained by Pruella as a thief. Hadn't it been the monkey that had ransacked her father's study and rifled through the papers at the Natural History Museum? What if...? "Can your monkey steal the Colonel's keys? said Polly, nudging Pruella's arm to get her attention.

"Keys...what are you talking about?"

Mussley sat up and squeaked, swishing his tail. The basu monkey stopped chattering and grinned.

"Oh, so you want me to help you, is that it?" sneered Pruella. "Why should I?"

"Surely that's pretty obvious," cut in Inspector Rington, a mass of squiggles now scrawled across his notebook.

"He could unlock this cage," said Polly. "You can't want to stay here?"

Then it occurred to Polly that maybe Pruella wanted to do just that. Polly had seen the way she had watched the goldicoots and the loopins and instantly Polly regretted her words.

Pruella shooed the basu monkey away, laughing.

"When will you ever learn?" sighed Madam Grunger, handing Polly a peppermint. Polly shook her head, she felt sick.

Minutes slipped into hours and the cramp in Polly's legs made her shift from side to side.

"Stop your wriggling," cursed Pruella.

Mussley crept onto Polly's lap. Pulling himself onto his hind legs he licked her face.

"Oh Mussley. I'm hungry too but I don't have anything to give you. Her tummy rumbled and she hugged him tightly.

"You'll catch something nasty," warned Madam Grunger, wrinkling her nose and shooing Mussley away. "Have you no idea how many germs an animal has on its tongue?" She wiped Polly's face with Inspector Rington's white handkerchief.

"Does anyone have a penknife or maybe a hair pin?" said Inspector Rington, reaching his long slender fingers through the bars of the cage and fiddling with the golden padlock.

Polly regretted abandoning her rucksack with the goat. She pictured the penknife tucked away in the side pocket. Madam Grunger reached into what was left of her French pleat and removed a silver hair pin.

"Aha, excellent!" exclaimed Inspector Rington. But just as he tried to twist the pin in the lock they heard footsteps heading towards them along the balcony.

"Colonel!" Pruella rattled the bars of the cage.

"Steady on," warned Inspector Rington almost landing on Madam Grunger's lap.

"Colonel, you and I have lots to talk about," called Pruella.

The cage began to swing and the Inspector's fingers slipped. The silver pin pinged out of his hand and skittered along the floor of the balcony out of reach.

"Look what you've done," said Inspector Rington.

"Listen to me, Colonel," persisted Pruella, standing now, her nose pressed up to the bars. The cage shifted unnervingly.

Madam Grunger groaned. "Oh do stop that." Her face had taken on a greenish tinge.

Colonel Brisket walked over to the cage. Polly was relieved to see there was no sign of his pistol but she wondered where her father was.

"At last," exclaimed Pruella.

The Colonel glared back at her although one of his eyes strayed beyond the cage as if it had a mind of its own. "I doubt we have anything to talk about, Pruella and you really must keep the noise down, the loopins have important work to do."

"You don't think the girl found you all by herself do you?"

Polly caught her breath. The goldicoot...had Pruella realised what Polly had herself, that surely her father must have sent the goldicoot to guide her?

"What do you mean by that?" spat the Colonel.

"Professor Gertram sent the goldicoot to show Polly the way here, that's what I mean. Why would he do that if he were your loyal partner?"

The Colonel's moustache bristled. "He did what? The traitor!"

Inspector Rington began scribbling in his notebook, muttering under his breath.

"Oh Polly," sighed Madam Grunger.

"You meddling little..." sneered the Colonel, standing so close to the bars that Polly could see spittle clinging to his moustache hairs.

Mussley leapt from Polly's lap, launching himself at the bars, baring his teeth.

"Get that thing away from me! How can you possibly know that?"

Pruella leaned in closer to the bars. "Let me out of here and I'll tell you all about it," she whispered, loud enough for Polly to hear.

Polly thought of the golden fob that sat in her pinafore pocket. What if the Colonel took it? She didn't dare touch it for fear of giving away its hiding place, though it seemed to glow warm in her pocket even as she thought about it.

The Colonel paused for a moment twiddling his moustache then he retrieved a bunch of keys from his pocket and proceeded to unlock the padlock. As the door swung open Mussley darted out and tore off down the wooden balcony, disappearing through the archway.

Chapter 25

"Mussley, come back!" Polly watched with dismay as Mussley scampered out of sight. "I have to get him back," she called, trying to squeeze through the cage after Pruella.

"Oh no you don't." The Colonel slammed the cage door shut, trapping Polly back inside.

"But... you can't just leave us here."

Colonel Brisket locked the cage. He spotted the silver pin on the floor and seized it. "Thought you'd get the better of me did you?"

"Now hang on there, Colonel, you can't imprison a member of her Majesty's constabulary." Inspector Rington pushed Madam Grunger out of his way and peered out at the Colonel, the Inspector's scrawny neck making him look more than ever like a caged turkey.

"My world, my rules," laughed the Colonel. "I'm the king here, or have you forgotten?" He pushed Pruella along in front of him.

"What about my father? Hasn't he got the guts to face me?" Polly's anger had grown over the hours she had sat squashed in the cage but even so she was a little shocked at how bitter she sounded. She felt abandoned, first by her father and then by Mussley, whose absence already felt like a hole growing inside her.

"We've a tight schedule and he's got work to do. We've lost quite enough time already. The steamship waits for no man and we need to be ready."

"Now look here, the authorities will take a very dim view of stolen gold, they'll sniff it out, just you see," said the Inspector, pushing his glasses back up his nose. "You'll never get the gold off the ship."

"Who cares about that," interrupted Madam Grunger. "Just look at the state of me. We're starving, filthy and frankly uncomfortable if you take my meaning, this is nothing short of kidnap." Madam Grunger grabbed hold of the Inspector's shoulder. "Some police officer you turned out to be. You should be doing something about this."

"Well madam, I would if..."

"Silence!"

The Colonel's roar was so loud even the goldicoot queen woke from her trance-like state and squawked, ruffling her feathers.

"England is not the only market eager for gold. The world awaits such treasures." The Colonel spread his arms wide and chuckled. "There are many countries that don't ask questions."

"Gold smuggling now is it?" piped up the Inspector. "Add to that theft and kidnap and you're looking at a heavy sentence, maybe even the gallows, along with all your associates of course." At this the Inspector glared at Pruella

159

who blatantly ignored him.

Polly let out a cry.

"No! But what about...?" Surely not her father? No matter how angry Polly was with him, however let down she felt, surely not that? Polly crumpled to the floor of the cage. Madam Grunger tried in vain to comfort her, her minty breath just made Polly's eyes sting with tears even more.

The Colonel opened his jacket revealing the pistol tucked into a leather holster strapped around his chest. "You have too much to say, Inspector."

The Inspector's eyebrow began to twitch and his skinny legs visibly shook. It was then that Polly heard a scurrying of feet. It was coming from the balcony directly above them. Straining to see, Polly caught a glimpse of fur, unmistakably that of Mussley's tail and beside him was the familiar tail of the basu monkey, curled high above its back. How extraordinary; what were they doing together?

The Colonel led Pruella away leaving Polly alone in the cage with Madam Grunger and Inspector Rington who were now no longer speaking to each other.

"Really!" Madam Grunger rummaged in her carpet bag.

"You'll have us off the ceiling if you rock us like that," said Inspector Rington. "What are you doing?"

"Looking for a way out of here of course," blustered Madam Grunger. "If you're not going to do anything, I will."

Polly watched as Madam Grunger began tossing things

out of her bag; a scarf, a black umbrella, a bag of humbugs and a rather smelly piece of newspaper wrapped up with string which reeked of rotten fish.

"There must be something," she muttered, pulling at something stuck in the corner. "Found it." Triumphantly Madam Grunger produced a burnished copper hair comb and raised it like a trophy above her head. "Will this do?"

Polly was so hungry she snatched up the bag of humbugs and popped two in her mouth at once. With the end of the umbrella she managed to push the offending piece of newspaper through the bars of the cage. What a pong! Polly recalled the figure she had seen sheltering outside the pawnbroker's. It had been wearing a floral scarf and held a wrapped newspaper parcel. Then she remembered the fish shop.

"You were following me!" cried Polly. "You both were."

"What does that matter now?" said Inspector Rington, who had prised a prong off of the hair comb and was twiddling it in the golden padlock.

Polly sat watching the goldicoot queen, quiet once more and majestic in all her golden plumage but yet so sad trapped in a tiny cage. She thought of all the birds caged in Pruella's zoo and Polly grew angrier still.

Three bent copper prongs later and still their cage was locked. Inspector Rington sat down beside Madam Grunger who was now snoring loudly and he sucked a humbug. Polly peered through the bars. If she stood on tiptoes she could just see the ground floor below her. It had grown dark outside and the lanterns cast an eerie light across the floor and up the walls. Polly shivered. Inspector Rington's head now rested on Madam Grunger's shoulder and though his mouth gaped open she was sure he was sound asleep. Polly had just decided to close her eyes too when she heard a whisper.

"Polly, can you hear me?"

Chapter 26

Polly peered into the darkness then she realised she was hearing the voice inside her head. The goldicoot!

"Where are you?"

The goldicoot swooped along the corridor, a glint of gold in the lamplight emerging out of the shadows. The bird flew straight towards her and seconds later came to land outside the cage where it stood staring in at her. It was the first time Polly had seen the goldicoot looking quite so intently at her. The bird put its head on one side. Her emerald eyes gleamed and its turquoise plume quivered. In her beak she held a key.

"I thought you'd forgotten about us," said Polly.

"The Colonel sleeps, we must leave now."

The goldicoot lowered its head and pushed the key through the bars of the cage. Madam Grunger began to stir but Inspector Rington was already on his feet.

"What the..."

"She won't hurt you," said Polly taking the key and unlocking the padlock.

"But..."

"I don't have time to explain," said Polly pushing the cage door open.

"At first the loopins didn't trust you."

Polly looked at the Inspector who looked back at her questioningly, his eyes wide at the sight of the goldicoot.

"Did you hear something?" said Polly.

"No, why, is someone coming?" Inspector Rington followed Polly out of the cage keeping his distance from the goldicoot.

So Polly really was the only one who could hear the goldicoot. She'd thought as much.

"I'm not like my father," said Polly. "Or Pruella."

"Who arc you talking to?" said Inspector Rington. IIe prodded Madam Grunger with the umbrella until at last she grunted awake.

"I know. Your father is in danger. We must go quickly."

"Why, what's happened?"

The goldicoot didn't reply. She spread her wings and took flight, gliding along the balcony back the way she had come.

"Oh do hurry up," said Inspector Rington, bundling Madam Grunger out of the cage. "Wait for us," he cried but Polly had set off after the goldicoot; she didn't want to let her out of her sight.

Inspector Rington and Madam Grunger ran after Polly.

"Quietly," hushed Polly.

Madam Grunger lagged behind, her cumbersome carpet bag slowing her down. If the goldicoot queen saw them she never acknowledged it. Polly ran down the golden staircase and out into the forest.

"I'm not sure my father deserves my help," called Polly, following the goldicoot who flew out towards the edge of the forest, to the golden waterfall.

"Maybe, maybe not."

Polly was still angry with her father but what Inspector Rington had said scared her. She couldn't imagine finding her father and then losing him forever.

In the moonlight the great bushes were huge shadows painted silver and the pool of molten gold lay dark and deeply mysterious but it was the sight of her father that stopped Polly in her tracks. A tall tree of twisted silver bark soared high into the night sky and dangling from its branches was a cage inside which was stuffed her father. The cage hung from a chain shackled around a branch and the tree trunk and then nailed into the ground. The cage was suspended precariously over the pool of molten gold.

"Father." The words were small in Polly's throat. She wondered where the Colonel slept and if Pruella was sleeping somewhere close by too. Polly's involuntary gasp was met by a tremble of leaves, a rustle of bushes and snap of a twig underfoot. Polly was sure she saw a shadow moving but when she looked again it was gone.

The goldicoot came to rest at the base of the tree.

"But why?" cried Polly.

"Pruella likes to talk."

"But we have to get him down." Polly strained to see her father. He was curled into a ball, lifeless from this distance and Polly suddenly felt sorry for him. She bet he'd never imagined that one day he would end up in a cage just like all the birds he'd caught. Maybe she should have felt he deserved it but she didn't. Having sat for hours in just such a cage Polly knew no one deserved that at all.

"Can't you help him?"

"Polly, are you talking to that bird?" The Inspector had caught up with her and stood wiping his brow with his now dirty handkerchief.

"Are you?" interrupted Madam Grunger, still trying to catch her breath.

"Of course I am," said Polly. "She led me here, helped father too." Turning once more to the goldicoot, Polly asked," Would the loopins help?"

"You'd have to ask them that yourself."

"But...how?"

"Talking to animals now are we?" Madam Grunger tutted. "That's absurd! Did your father put such a ridiculous idea into your head? I warned him no good would come from encouraging you."

The goldicoot beat her wings and flew away from the tree, out beyond the golden waterfall to a large white rock which sat beside the pool of molten gold. She gestured to a smaller white boulder between two bigger rocks.

"Under there, but only you."

Much to Madam Grunger's outrage, Polly ignored her and ran over to the white boulder which she easily rolled aside. Beneath it she found a large hole, the entrance to some kind of tunnel and Polly was small enough to squeeze inside. She heard a squeak, just like Mussley's and as she lowered herself into the tunnel she felt the softness of his fur against her hand but when she called out to Mussley he wasn't there. Polly couldn't help remembering the myriad of tunnels that had led her here and the beast that roamed within. Maybe this was a trap after all?

Chapter 27

It was several minutes before Polly's eyes adjusted and she
realised she was sitting in a tunnel in cool shifting sand. She
heard the sound of chattering, like a group of monkeys in the
distance and she was about to try to get up when something
soft and furry landed on her head, scooted down her front and
into her lap.

"Mussley, you scared me."

She squeezed him tightly. "I thought you'd deserted me."

Mussley squeaked excitedly. Jumping down from her lap
he scurried down the tunnel, his paws sinking into the soft
sand. A flickering light lit the tunnel and she could hear the
sound of water. Surely she wasn't far from the waterfall
somewhere above her but this sounded different, like water
lapping onto a beach. The sand crunched beneath her boots.

"Slow down, Mussley."

When she caught up with him he was standing at the
water's edge watching a group of loopins loading a canoe with
golden trunks. On hearing Polly, the loopin holding the canoe
steady looked up. The creature's fur was dazzlingly white
against the turquoise of the water. Polly was surprised to find
she was standing in a cavern, an underground lagoon that was
brightly lit by burning torches set around the walls of rock
casting a blaze of light across the ripples of the water. Polly

had no idea if the loopins could understand her but she had to try.

"I need your help," she called.

The loopin, a collar of sapphires around its neck, flicked its tail high above its head. It opened its mouth and let out a cry, so shrill it hurt Polly's ears.

"Please, my father...he's..." What could she say to defend her father? Yes he was a hunter but even she knew he wasn't like the Colonel. So she said what mattered the most, even if the loopin couldn't understand. "He's my father."

The loopin had already gone back to loading the canoe. The others jumped aboard, tapping the side of the canoe impatiently.

"Wait, I can help you," said Polly. "If you help my father...I could stop the Colonel."

The loopin let out a terrific screech, so loud that Mussley clung to Polly's ankles. Was he laughing at her? The screech echoed around the cavern. The loopin's eyes burned bright. It opened its hand and there in his blue palm lay a golden fob, just like the one the goldicoot had given Polly. The loopin tapped it and watched the dials spin around then clasped it between its fingers and flew into the canoe which had already started moving. The canoe rowed away from the lagoon and down a narrow stretch of water which flowed into a tunnel taking the loopins and their canoe out of sight.

Polly picked up Mussley. "Did you see that? I knew they

must have made the golden fob. I wish they'd understood me."

Mussley squeaked. He wriggled until Polly let him down and he raced back the way they had come.

By the time Polly found the hole again and pulled herself up after Mussley she was sure Madam Grunger and Inspector Rington would have given up waiting but there they still stood. Carefully Polly replaced the boulder and made her way back to the others.

"How dare you run off like that," blustered Madam Grunger.

"We really shouldn't be out in the open like this," said Inspector Rington. He leaned towards Polly. "I rather think these trees have eyes. What if the Colonel finds us...what then?"

Above them Polly's father stirred in the cage. She wanted to call out to him but she daren't. In the stillness of the night her very words would echo. Even now the Colonel could be on his way.

"Where's the goldicoot?" she whispered.

"Never mind that bird, we have to get out of here," whispered Madam Grunger. "Leave the Professor, there's nothing we can do. We must..."

"We can make our way back to the tunnel to the rainforest, I noted down some directions." The Inspector took out his note book and flicked through the pages. By the light of the moon Polly was surprised how well she could see. She heard a rustling behind her and was about to cry out when she recognised the silhouette of the goat, it was carrying the basu monkey on its back. A shadow swooped overhead.

"You must hide."

The goldicoot glided above her.

"But where?"

"That's enough of this nonsense," huffed Madam Grunger. "You come with me, my girl and..."

"No, I won't," cried Polly. Her voice made the trees shudder. No matter how much she hated what her father had done she couldn't just leave him there, like that.

"Follow me quickly."

"We can't talk here, you have to follow me." Polly beckoned the Inspector to follow her. Madam Grunger gave a deep resigned sigh and snatched up her carpet bag.

"We need to formulate a viable plan," panted Inspector Rington, running now to keep up with Polly and Mussley who darted into the cover of the trees, following the goldicoot to the place where the trees grew so densely that Polly could barely see where she was going. She followed the goldicoot blindly, snatches of moonlit feathers leading the three of them deep into the forest.

When at last the goldicoot landed on a fallen tree Polly was out of breath. Madam Grunger had turned crimson and was struggling to catch her breath. The inspector collapsed onto the forest floor, wheezing.

Polly stood inches away from the goldicoot. The great golden bird blinked its turquoise eyes at her. Polly reached out a hand and touched the bird's head. The goldicoot closed its eyes.

"My name is Goldermare."

"Thank you, Goldermare, for saving us." Polly sat down beside Goldermare and let Mussley curl up on her lap.

"What are the loopins? They have golden fobs, just like the one you wanted me to have."

"Loopins are navigators. They explore the tunnels which lay hidden beneath the Hibrodean rainforest. Our world may be home to the gold of life but it is by no means the only world."

Polly couldn't believe what she was hearing.

"It is a secret the Colonel must never be allowed to know."

Chapter 28

Polly was overcome by tiredness so heavy it swamped her like a wool blanket. Goldermare slept, her head under her wing. Madam Grunger snored loudly, her head resting on Inspector Rington's chest. Polly slept fitfully, her dreams punctuated by the cry of the goldicoots and the sound of a pistol firing.

Crack!

Polly sat up. Another gunshot rang out.

"Father!"

A rush of wings overhead heralded the arrival of a flock of goldicoots. Goldermare was awake and in the air in seconds.

"The Colonel has discovered your escape."

The goldicoots swarmed around the clearing, the tone of their cries as terrified as the thoughts racing through Polly's mind.

"What's happening?" shouted Polly.

"Surely that much is obvious," snapped Madam Grunger, clambering up off the ground and smoothing down her bloomers, brushing twigs from the sleeve of her blouse.

"Well, are you going to tell me?" Polly stamped her feet. "Is it Father?"

"The Colonel is angry, so very angry."

"Show me," shouted Polly, fearing the worst. "I'm not a

child, I need to know."

Without waiting for an answer Polly sprinted through the trees back towards the waterfall, Goldermare flying above her head.

"Come back. Come back this instant!" bellowed Madam Grunger.

"You're doing just what the Colonel wants you to do," called Inspector Rington, chasing after her.

Mussley streaked out in front.

"If the Colonel so much as touches my father I'll..." Polly stopped, her words hanging unspoken in the air. Through the trees she could already see. Her father's cage was no longer suspended high above the pool of molten gold but now hung just above its surface. If her father reached out a hand it would surely touch the liquid gold.

"No..he wouldn't..."

"Wouldn't he?" puffed Madam Grunger. She grabbed hold of Polly and pulled her close. "There is nothing you could have done. Your father would want me to take you away from here this minute."

"Let me go...no he wouldn't...what would you know? I came this far on my own and I'm not leaving without him."

"Fine words, fine words indeed, very commendable," said Inspector Rington. "But for once I agree with Madam Grunger. You must leave this criminal to the hands of the law, it's time for us to leave."

"I can't and I won't. Goldermare, you have to help me, help me free him before…"

"Stop talking to that bird, do you hear me and listen to me…"

But Polly pushed herself free from Madam Grunger's hold.

"Help my father, Goldermare, you must."

Above her Goldermare flapped her golden wings.

"I will help you, if you free our queen."

All the hot air of enthusiasm which had filled Polly's lungs sunk in that second. The goldicoot queen. Of course, the reason the goldicoots, and the loopins for that matter, let the Colonel tread all over them. How could Polly ever rescue the goldicoot queen? Polly's frustration bit hard inside her and she wanted to cry. Surely there had to be a way to free the goldicoot queen. It couldn't be that difficult, could it?

Chapter 29

From the safety of the trees Polly watched the Colonel. He stomped up and down touting his pistol, waiting. Well she wasn't going to give him the satisfaction of catching her. Maybe the inspector was right, on that point anyway. Polly didn't have a plan as such but there wasn't any time to thrash out the details. If she was going to release the queen of the goldicoots it would have to be now.

"I know you think I should leave here, run away as fast as I can but I can't." Polly spoke slowly and carefully. She had to seem in control, she knew that. "If we can free the goldicoot's queen, the goldicoots and maybe even the loopins may help us free my father. But we need to act now."

Madam Grunger sucked her teeth. Inspector Rington paced up and down, his hands clenched behind his back. "A plan, yes very good. I see the logic. This could work."

"Us, a rescue party? Don't be absurd." Madam Grunger stared at Polly. "Do I look like one?"

Standing in her bloomers with a carpet bag in one hand and a shabby umbrella keeping off the morning sun in the other, Madam Grunger didn't look like a soldier or a freedom fighter but she did look formidable. What she lacked in skills she definitely made up for in bulk.

"Mussley, find the monkey. If anyone can steal a tool to

break open a lock he can. Madam Grunger, you can haul the cage down and Inspector Rington, you're look out."

Mussley squeaked loudly and ran out into the forest.

"Follow me," called Polly, striding back to where the giant tree stood and the queen of the goldicoots hung in her cage.

"Now look here," piped up the Inspector. "When the Colonel realises what we're doing how do you propose I fend off a man with a pistol?"

Polly had thought about nothing but the pistol ever since she heard it but she had no answer for that, though she didn't want to admit it. "You'll think of something," she said, racing ahead.

The goldicoots kept close, with Goldermare in the lead but once Polly and the others reached the giant tree the goldicoots settled in the trees and there they waited.

"Have you seen the size of that cage?" huffed Madam Grunger as she lumbered up the golden staircase after Polly.

"At least there's only one way in," said Inspector Rington. "I'll stay here at the top of the staircase and give the alarm if I see the Colonel coming." The Inspector grabbed the umbrella from Madam Grunger and held it out like a sword, swishing it from side to side. "He'll have to get past me first, that will slow him down."

Polly stood on the balcony. She could see the goldicoot queen in her cage suspended from the ceiling above them. She seemed lifeless and so very still. Mussley bounded along the balcony accompanied now by the basu monkey who was trailing a long piece of golden rope, clutching a gold poker between its teeth as it ran.

"Brilliant idea!" exclaimed Polly, realising she hadn't thought how they were going to reach the cage.

Mussley squeaked bossily and the basu monkey chattered excitedly, dropping the golden poker by Polly's feet. The monkey sprinted along the top of the bannister of the balcony before launching himself at the cage.

Madam Grunger went white, swaying on her feet and Polly really thought she might actually faint. The golden rope swept across the void in the monkey's grasp and for a few seconds time seemed to go in slow motion. With a screech of triumph, the basu monkey landed on the top of the golden cage.

"Bravo!" called the Inspector, waving his umbrella.

Madam Grunger breathed again.

"Tie it on," called Polly, reaching over the balcony. "Now throw the other end to me."

"You'll fall if you lean that far," bellowed Madam Grunger, grabbing hold of Polly's legs in a bear hug.

Outside came a great commotion; the flapping of wings and a loud squawk. It could only mean one thing. The Colonel was coming.

"Throw me the rope," cried Polly.

The basu monkey lassoed the rope but just as Polly tried

to grasp it the rope slipped through her fingers.

"I'll fend the Colonel off as long as I can,"cried the inspector.

Mussley squeaked.

"Throw it again," cried Polly. "Get ready, Madam Grunger."

This time the basu monkey threw the rope and Polly caught it. Madam Grunger wrapped it around her wide girth and braced herself to pull the cage towards the balcony.

"No you don't!" Colonel Brisket stood at the bottom of the staircase, his moustache twitching with rage.

"I rather think you need to hurry," called the Inspector, raising the umbrella out in front of him, his legs astride like a rather spindly samurai warrior preparing for battle.

"Heave!" called Polly. "You can do it."

Madam Grunger braced herself against the bannister and heaved the rope with all her might. Slowly but surely the cage was pulled nearer to where Polly stood waiting to grab hold of it.

"Stand down or I'll shoot!" bellowed the Colonel.

"Keep pulling, nearly there," called Polly, her legs and arms shaking so much she feared she may collapse at the vital moment.

The Colonel bounded up the staircase, his pistol raised. "Don't make me use it."

The Inspector swished the umbrella faster and faster.

"Oh do stop that," shouted the Colonel. "It won't help you."

The cage was moving and it swung so close to Polly's outstretched arms that she could see the pupils of the goldicoot queen and every delicate golden strand of her feathers but she just wasn't close enough to reach.

Mussley let out a terrifically long screech and the basu monkey clapped his hands and sprinted down the steps towards the Colonel.

The Colonel raised his pistol to fire just as the basu monkey jumped, forcing the Colonel to lower his arm.

The pistol shot rang out, missing the Inspector entirely and embedding itself into one of the golden steps.

The basu monkey clung tightly to the Colonel's neck and the Colonel had to drop the pistol to prise the monkey's fingers away from his eyes.

"One last pull, Madam Grunger!" cried Polly, but deep down she knew it would never be enough. The cage was just too heavy. Madam Grunger was sweating profusely, holding fast to the rope but the cage wouldn't move any closer even when Polly tried to tug the rope herself.

"I'm sorry," blurted Madam Grunger, letting go of the rope. "It's no good."

The golden cage swung back to where it had started, with the goldicoot queen still prisoner. Polly wanted to cry.

Mussley shot down the steps and raced to where the pistol

lay but the Colonel flung off the basu monkey and kicked the pistol out of Mussley's reach, kicking Mussley as he did so.

Mussley yelped.

"Leave Mussley alone," said Polly.

"Now look here," said Inspector Rington, squaring up to the Colonel so that they were face to face on the top step. "Let's be civil about this."

The Colonel bent down and retrieved his pistol. "Out of my way!"

The Colonel shoved the Inspector aside and thundered over to where Polly sat slumped next to Madam Grunger. "You're no better than your father." Colonel Brisket bent down and sneered in Polly's face. "You belong together."

The basu monkey ventured too near and the Colonel, catching sight of him with his wayward eye, swiped him up by his tail, dangling him upside down.

"And as for you, you filthy vermin, a cage is too good for you."

Madam Grunger did something Polly never would have imagined possible. She stood up and grabbed the monkey right out of the Colonel's hands and stuffed it into the safety of her carpet bag. "You can leave him alone, you overinflated bully."

The Colonel sucked in his breath and was clearly about to retaliate when another voice filled the air.

"Missed all the fun have I?"

Pruella.

"Playing the hero are we, Polly?" Pruella jeered from the staircase.

Mussley snarled.

"I hope you won't put up with this, Colonel. Such behaviour deserves punishment indeed."

The Colonel swung to face her.

"What's it to do with you?"

"Come, come Colonel, we're partners, are we not?"

The Colonel grunted.

"Come on, Inspector, we can't have you meddling. Time is of the essence. We have a ship to catch and a schedule to stick to."

Chapter 30

Molten gold glimmered in the morning sun just inches away from Polly's feet. If she reached out a finger and dipped it into the gold, so thick and smooth like paint, would her finger really turn to solid gold?

"I never truly believed you would come looking for me."

Polly's father crouched beside her, her fellow prisoner, their fate hanging in the balance just like the cage that now housed them. It swayed disconcertingly whenever Polly tried to change position.

"Surely you know I can't resist a puzzle?" said Polly. "It was poor Mundle, clearly traumatised and with mysterious injuries that convinced me there was more to your disappearance than just carelessness in the rainforest. Oh and the break in at home of course and the theft at the Natural History Museum..."

"My...what a lot has been happening since I left. That explains Inspector Rington at least, we were so careful to cover our tracks. But Mundle...I wondered what happened to him. It was my fault of course. I wasn't completely honest with him about my expedition but then I didn't really believe in the beast that Edmund Milner described, well not until..."

Polly remembered finding the remains of Premble and shuddered.

"You should have told me," said Polly. "We never had secrets, not before Mother died."

"Sometimes we make bad choices, decisions we later regret. I've let you both down. Times were difficult and there was never enough money. I rather think I was taken in by my brother. It was such a wonderful quest, a magnificent prize."

"But you were killing birds for money...making me believe your lies...I'm...disappointed. I should have believed Madam Grunger."

"I know you are and I'm sorry. Gold made a fool of me, of all of us."

In the silence that followed, Polly stared out across the golden pool to the waterfall. The goldicoots filled the sky, flying in formation from the entrance to the mine, carrying baskets brimming with gemstones of every colour, under the watchful eye of the Colonel. Beside the pool, loopins were building a second wooden cart. The first was already half full of golden boxes, goblets and bowls. Pruella stood with her trousers rolled up around her ankles helping to unload a small wooden canoe on the nearby river. A loopin passed her golden candlesticks and plates. In the glint of the sun Polly could see Pruella was wearing something around her neck, rubies as red as blood.

"It didn't take Pruella long to choose sides," said Polly's father. "I always guessed she was more interested in money than the animals in her zoo."

Polly couldn't help feeling guilty about her mother's ring which she had pawned. No amount of gemstones or gold could ever replace the last thing of her mother's and now it was gone and all Polly's hopes with it. And for what? She couldn't bear for anything to happen to her father, not after everything she'd been through but she couldn't forgive him either. Could she?

"I know you're mad at me, Polly but believe me, seeing you was the best thing ever. It made me realise what I so nearly lost. I am so very proud of you, Polly. And you have made me laugh. Who'd have ever thought of Madam Grunger in the rainforest?"

Polly found herself laughing, she couldn't help it.

"Does the Colonel really think he can drag all of that back through the tunnels, with the beast? That beast ate Premble!"

"Crikey!" Polly's father put his arm around her. "The beast wouldn't have been half as angry if the Colonel hadn't shot its mate. Such a magnificent animal, such a waste. He says that after this first shipment he'll blast a new tunnel through to the rainforest with dynamite. I've never seen my brother so determined, so driven, and by what?"

Greed, though Polly sadly.

"Where do you think the Colonel has taken Madam Grunger and Inspector Rington?"

"They won't be far," said Polly's father. "I doubt he'd harm them, not really."

"How can you be so sure?"

"Well...I guess I can't."

At least Mussley escaped, and the basu monkey, thanks to Madam Grunger, thought Polly.

"But I don't see how we're going to get out of here." Polly's father lowered his head but she was sure she saw a tear in his eye.

Squeak! Squeak!

"Mussley, is that you?"

Beside the golden pool, Polly could just see him sitting up on his hind legs and beside him sat the basu monkey, clapping his hands. There was the sound of rustling and the goat appeared from behind a bush.

I wonder, thought Polly.

Chapter 31

The hours dragged by and the afternoon sun made Polly terrifically thirsty. Her father seemed to have given up hope and dozed off beside her, snoring gently. Polly watched Colonel Brisket and Pruella load the second cart and when it was fully laden the pair headed back to the waterfall.

"You can't just leave us here," called Polly.

The Colonel stopped walking. "Your father made his choice and you are clearly not to be trusted."

"At least let us down from here," Polly pleaded.

Polly's father, hearing Polly's cries, sat up. "She's just a child, let her go."

The Colonel removed his field hat and wiped his brow. He looked puffed up and red and Polly noticed his pistol tucked into his belt. Pruella paused and took a metal flask from a backpack over her shoulder. She took a long glug, her arm now jangling with gold bangles.

"It won't be long now. We leave at sunrise but before we do I'll have you lowered into the gold. What better deterrent for the over curious than solid gold statues, here forever for all to see? Maybe I should get your friends to join you. I could put you all in a gold cage. What a fitting tribute for a hunter."

"But..." spluttered Polly's father, holding her tight. "You can't do that..."

"I think you'll find a king can. I owe all this to you, for which I am grateful, of course, brother."

With that the Colonel and Pruella continued on their way back to the forest, not once looking back.

Polly's father hugged her tightly. She felt a tear on her cheek, wet and warm. Well, Polly wasn't going to just wait to be turned into gold, not when there was still something she could do.

"Goldermare!"

The goldicoots were nowhere to be seen. They'd flown back to the forest hours ago but Polly kept calling.

"She can't help you." Polly's father took her hand. "She wouldn't dare."

"But I can get us out of here, I know I can and without suspicion falling on the goldicoots. Just let me try."

"Polly, it took courage and resourcefulness for you to find me but you can't get us down from here."

Polly felt an anger swell inside her. Father was wrong. She clenched her fists and in her mind she thought over and over:

"Goldermare, you have to find Mussley. I know he's there somewhere waiting. Please Goldermare."

Polly knew Mussley was anything but ordinary and somehow he knew what she was saying, had an affinity with her like she'd never felt before and now she really needed him.

A few moments later when even Polly was beginning to

think there was nothing she could do, Goldermare answered her.

"Mussley is on his way. You need only think what you want to say to me and I will hear you."

Polly jumped up, making the cage swing alarmingly.

"Sit down, Polly, or you'll have us in even sooner."

The sun crept below the horizon and shadows threw themselves across the grass between the bushes.

"Mussley will get us down."

Her father smiled. "I'm sure he loves you but even Mussley can't get us down from here, no matter how much he may want to."

"Who said anything about Mussley doing it alone? Animals are ingenious and very resourceful, something you have failed to realise. Just you wait."

"Don't get your hopes up, Polly. You've come so far but some things just aren't possible."

"That's where you're wrong. They may seem like it because you don't believe. Well I do. Mussley!"

Seconds later Mussley trotted up to the golden pool followed by the goat, with the basu monkey riding on its back.

"Oh Mussley, I knew you'd come. Get us out of here."

The goat beat the ground with its hoof and the basu monkey chattered excitedly.

"What the…"

"Mussley, you need to get the monkey to steal the key. I just hope the goat is strong enough."

"What are you suggesting?" called Polly's father, sitting up now staring at Mussley, the goat and the basu monkey who seemed to be listening to every word Polly was saying.

"You impressed the loopins with your attempt to save our queen. They trust you."

"Will they help me?"

"Who are you talking to, Polly?"

"Goldermare, of course."

"They are ready and waiting."

"How on earth do you think that lot will get us out of here?" asked her father.

"Just you wait and see," said Polly, her excitement growing.

Mussley squeaked in agreement and the basu monkey clapped its hands.

Chapter 32

Before the moon was high in the sky the goat trotted into the clearing by the golden pool leading a motley band of rescuers. A dozen loopins followed Mussley who was sitting high on the goat's back with the basu monkey beside him brandishing a golden key.

"And there's me thinking your plan was a crazy fantasy," laughed Polly's father.

He watched in astonishment as the loopins unhitched the rope that held the cage suspended below the tree and then tied it around the goat's chest. With an almighty heave the goat pulled, snorting with the effort until at last the cage jolted and began to move. The loopins had formed a chain and together they helped the goat take the weight. They tugged and tugged, hoisting the cage higher and higher, inch by inch. It wasn't long before the cage had left the golden pool far below. The cage wavered, swaying high in the tree's branches.

"Stop, Mussley," called Polly, steadying herself as she stood up.

"Absolutely amazing," gasped her father.

The basu monkey, the key clenched between his teeth, scampered up the tree, leaping from branch to branch before landing on top of the cage, peering down at Polly inside.

"Thank you," said Polly, taking the key from the monkey's

191

mouth and reaching through the bars to unlock the padlock.

"I hope you're good at climbing, Father, it's the only way down."

And so it was that by moonlight, Polly and her father clambered out of the cage, along the branch and carefully scrambled back down the tree to solid ground. Polly's legs felt all wibbly and weak from being cramped for so long but she was relieved to have left the golden pool behind her.

"Oh Mussley." She scooped him up and Mussley licked her face all over. "I'm pleased to see you too."

The loopins let out a high pitched screech.

"And thank you too," laughed Polly.

"Who would have thought it possible," sighed her father. "Maybe instead of taking Mundle I should have taken you as my assistant."

Polly gave her father a hard stare.

"I know, I know, I should never have come."

But despite everything that had happened Polly couldn't have imagined never meeting Mussley or Goldermare.

"Madam Grunger…the Inspector! We have to try to find them. I feel rather sorry for Madam Grunger, she's not exactly cut out for the rainforest."

"Oh I don't know, she's rather surprised me," said Polly's father, stroking Mussley's head.

The loopins opened their wings, leapt into the air and started flying back towards the forest. Polly untied the goat and gave chase, Mussley racing along ahead of her.

"I think the loopins know where they are," called Polly, her legs soon gaining strength.

"Wait for me," called her father.

Despite the moonlight it was dark between the trees and Polly realised that somewhere ahead the Colonel and Pruella slept and the rescue was far from over. She stumbled on a fallen branch and down she fell with a crash!

"Polly," called her father.

"Ouch, I've twisted my ankle." Polly's ankle throbbed and up ahead she thought she heard someone call out but maybe it was just the wind that now whipped through the trees, tossing her hair into her eyes.

"I've got you," said her father, helping her up.

Ahead of them, where the path began to narrow, stood a large tree that Polly hadn't noticed before. A door in its trunk stood ajar, letting light spill into the forest.

"Shhh!" whispered her father. "They're probably sleeping. I'll take a look inside, you wait here. The Colonel will probably be in the goldicoot's palace but keep a look out.

The loopins sat high in the branches above, silently waiting. Their white coats had taken on a bluish hue under the light of the moon. Mussley sat very still, his ears alert. Even the basu monkey made no sound as her father tiptoed into the tree.

Polly waited, the air now holding a chill that made her

shiver. Inside she could hear whispering. It sounded like Madam Grunger talking. Polly crept nearer to listen. There came a snap of a twig behind her and Polly swung round and came face to face with Pruella. Her silvery hair was plaited around her neck, her eyes an icy green, her hand held steady holding a pistol aimed straight at Polly.

"Thought you'd sneak in here and let that silly old lady and the constable out did you? Well think again."

Madam Grunger came bundling out of the door closely followed by Inspector Rington and Polly's father. Polly let out a warning cry.

Pruella raised the pistol high above her head and pulled the trigger.

The shot rang out into the trees. There was a terrific rustling of leaves as the loopins leapt from the trees in a panic.

A flash of gold was followed by another as goldicoots swooped overhead.

Pruella fired again and this time a golden bird plummeted to the forest floor and there it lay, lifeless, its legs stuck up in the air. A single drop of gold oozed onto the ground, like gold paint expelled from a tube.

"No!" cried Polly." What if that were Goldermare?

Chapter 33

Polly knelt down and stroked the dead goldicoot's beak. She felt its loss like a bullet to the heart and it was all her fault. If she hadn't followed her father into the Hibrodean rainforest none of this would have happened.

The loopins shrieked, leaping from branch to branch in such a frenzy that leaves fell like it was a gale in autumn. Polly shed a tear that trickled down her cheek and dripped from her chin.

"Now get away from the tree where I can see you, all of you." Pruella jabbed the pistol in the air.

A mighty clatter of footsteps through the forest brought Colonel Brisket with them, his hair sticking out at angles, his shirt buttoned lopsidedly and with a mood as foul as Pruella's deeds.

"What is it with you!" he bellowed, glaring at Polly. "I've always said children are nasty, foul creatures that should never be born. Give me that, you crazy woman!" The Colonel snatched the pistol away from Pruella.

"But..."

"Don't you ever think?"

"It's just a bird...I was..."

"This is my operation, mine, do you hear me? We need the goldicoots' co-operation. We had an understanding before you..."

"Just let us go," interrupted Polly's father.

Colonel Brisket puffed out his chest, his bloodshot eyes bulging. "I am king here, me, do you hear me? As my little brother, you have shown yourself incapable of getting the job done but you still have work to do. You're going to pull those carts through the tunnels to the rainforest. I need something to distract the beast. As for you..." The Colonel spat at Pruella. "Tie those three up and keep an eye on them. I rather think watching them walk the plank would be much more fun, don't you?"

"Now look here," blustered Madam Grunger, pushing past Pruella. "I never trusted you, you always had your hand in the cookie jar."

"Hurry up with that rope Pruella, unless you want to join them."

"Don't think Her Majesty's Constabulary will stop looking for me. I shouldn't wonder if they haven't travelled to the Hibrodean rainforest already."

"Well Inspector, if they're as ineffectual as you I shan't have any trouble, shall I?"

Colonel Brisket crouched down and plucked up Mussley, squeezing him tightly around his tummy. "As for your little friends...no one makes a fool out of me."

*

Daybreak brought with it a blistering heat. The wind of the

night before vanished and without any respite from the sun, Polly, Madam Grunger and Inspector Rington stood roped together by the edge of the golden pool, the waterfall gushing before them. Poor Mussley and the basu monkey sat hunched in a small bamboo cage and even the goat had been shackled to the bottom of the tree beside the pool. So much for the rescue party, her ingenious animals and her bravado, if that was what it was, because now it felt like a stupid child's game. It would be almost as ridiculous as Colonel Brisket's game if it weren't so horribly real. He stood wearing his gold crown, encrusted in emeralds, a heavy gold chain weighting down his neck like a town crier. If it really was the same uncle that had shared their Christmas dinner more than once, he didn't look the same any more. If pure evil had a look, he had it.

As for her father, in that split second as she watched him strapping the heavy load to the cart with Pruella, she saw the father she'd always loved and still did. A father who, as he admitted, had made mistakes but was still her father. What if the beast ate him, just like Premble? Though of course she wouldn't be there to see it as she would have been dipped in gold and would never see again.

The loopins kept their distance but she could feel their eyes watching her as Colonel Brisket carried a plank of wood and laid it out so it stretched across the golden pool, one end firmly weighted by a heavy boulder that he had struggled to roll. Polly idly wondered if the plank would take Madam

Grunger's weight or if it would snap in two as she walked across it.

The goldicoots were nowhere to be seen. They were angry and scared and she couldn't blame them but more than anything Polly wanted to say goodbye to Goldermare. She remembered what Goldermare said to her. *You can always talk to me, just think the words in your head.*

So Polly did.

"Goldermare, where are you?"

"You first," growled Colonel Brisket, grabbing hold of Inspector Rington's arm. He untied his hands and pushed him onto the plank.

It was like a cruel game of pirates, only in this game, the treasure would kill them.

"I shan't," replied Inspector Rington.

"No!" cried Polly's father, but Pruella already had the pistol on him.

Colonel Brisket shoved the Inspector so hard he stumbled and fell, perilously close to the edge of the plank. His glasses fell from his nose and toppled into the liquid gold with a glug!

Polly's heart seemed to stop at that moment and with all the will in her body she said the words over and over in her head:

"Help us Goldermare."

If they could hear her they would come, Polly was sure of

it. They wouldn't stand by, not now.

"Help us Goldermare."

Inspector Rington scrambled up, a bruise swelling on his lip.

"Goldermare you must come now."

Chapter 34

"I don't have the time for this, Inspector." Colonel Brisket grabbed hold of Inspector Rington's arm.

The stillness of the morning broke with the sound of birds' wings beating the air. Horrified, the Colonel turned to see a ginormous flock of goldicoots heading his way, their golden feathers glinting in the sun. He shielded his eyes from the glare.

"Goldermare!" cried Polly.

Flying in an arrowhead formation, with Goldermare at the helm, the goldicoots aimed straight for where the Colonel stood, his usually ruddy face bleached as white as a loopin's fur.

Pruella, startled by the rush of wings, looked away from Professor Gertram. It was her first mistake, for in that second the Professor grabbed the pistol from her hand and threw it far across the grass, where it landed close to a flowering bush.

"Polly!"

The goldicoots were upon the Colonel in minutes, swarming around him in a frenzy. All Polly could see were his arms thrashing against them. His screams filled the air.

"Untie me," called Polly to the Inspector, who simply couldn't believe his eyes. He looked so different without his glasses as he fumbled with the knot. Free at last Polly raced over to the bamboo cage and released the catch. Mussley shot out followed by the basu monkey who shrieked with excitement and chased across the grass.

Professor Gertram threw his arms around Polly, relief painted all across his face. "I thought..."

"Hey, you'll squash me," said Polly. "Looks like the Colonel's got his hands full."

Colonel Brisket, now prostrate on the ground, fought with his fists and his feet but he stood little chance under the weight of gold that pinned him down. His crown tumbled from his head, where it lay sparkling in the sun.

"What about Pruella?" said Polly.

"Looks like the little madam's getting out when she can," said Madam Grunger, guiding Inspector Rington away from the golden pool, her face red and puffy, her bloomers now decidedly grubby. "And as for you Professor, you owe me more than my month's wages...you have no idea what I have had to do..."

"Madam Grunger, I can never thank you enough, you're worth your weight in gold."

"That's not funny," snapped Madam Grunger but even Polly saw her smile, it was such a rare sight to behold.

"Trust Pruella," said Polly's father.

Pruella in her panic grabbed handfuls of jewels and trinkets from the cart and stuffed them down her top and in her pockets. With one last look in Polly's direction, Pruella ran away from the waterfall in the direction of tunnel back to the rainforest.

"Let her go," said Polly's father. "Did you do this?" He nodded towards where the Colonel lay. A single goldicoot swooped overhead and out above Polly, flying so low that she could see Goldermare's emerald eyes. Polly smiled.

"You have Goldermare to thank for that."

"I doubt Pruella will get far."

"Do you mean the beast?"

"Oh she has a chance against the beast, I meant the goldicoot's curse."

There was a noise behind them.

"I wonder where the loopins are?" said Polly, looking around her.

"Over there," cried her father, pointing towards the forest.

Sure enough, a band of loopins chased towards them, their pearlescent wings shimmering, their feet pounding the ground, their tails raised high. A huge shadow spread across them.

The goldicoot queen.

She flew through the air, her immense wingspan outstretched, her turquoise plume like a crown upon her head. Polly watched in awe as the queen swept over the golden pool, skimming the top of the molten gold, drinking deeply from its depths. The brilliance of her feathers grew with each drop of gold. She soared above them, circling once, twice, before swooping down to where the Colonel lay. She plucked the crown up in her beak and carried it high above the golden pool where she released it from her talons. The crown fell, spinning in the air and then it was swallowed beneath the surface.

"No one steals from the goldicoots. Death is our curse."

Polly heard the words clearly in her head but they were so different, they couldn't have been the words of Goldermare but of the goldicoot queen herself.

"What do you mean, the curse of the goldicoot?" said Polly aloud.

"It kills those who dare steal the goldicoot's gold," replied her father. "Remember Edmund Milner? If it hadn't been for that gold leaf..."

"But how do you know?" Polly was sure her father hadn't heard the goldicoot queen.

Polly's father retrieved a folded piece of paper from his breast pocket and handed it to her.

"It's the last page of Edmund Milner's journal. I never showed it to my brother, there would have been no stopping him anyway and I...well, I didn't really think I believed in it...not until now anyway."

Polly opened the piece of paper, written in the same handwriting as the pages she had stolen from Pruella.

As I lie with a fever I cannot hope to control, I keep hearing the same words...they haunt my nightmares, break into my waking thoughts... "You can never escape the curse of the goldicoot until there's not a living breath left in your body.

"Well I doubt Pruella will escape the curse."

As if on cue Pruella darted back towards the waterfall, spraying gold trinkets as she ran, her eyes as haunted as Edmund Milner's words, the beast close behind her.

Chapter 35

Smoke billowed from the beast's nostrils. Its head was as regal as an eagle, its two legs solid as tree trunks, coated in the coarse hair of a lion and ending in huge paws with claws razor sharp and drawn. The beast towered above Pruella, who ran like a hare in the sight of a gun, first one way and then another. But her panicked turns were no match for the beast, whose legs were not only strong but fast like a wild cat chasing its prey across the prairie.

Polly watched in horror as poor Pruella, exhausted, cowered behind a large bush, as if its foliage could really hide her from view.

"The beast!" cried Polly's father. "I really think it might…"

"I can't look," cut in Madam Grunger, "and neither should a child." She bundled Polly to her chest.

"We have to help her," said Polly, wriggling free. "Maybe we could distract it?"

But even Polly knew it was too late for that. The beast opened its beak and a terrific roar of fire burnt the bush to a crisp. The flames licked the air, smoke twisting and turning, all that was left of Pruella's hiding place.

Pruella, her hair singed and her face blackened, ran faster than Polly had ever seen anyone run before but the beast was right behind her as she sprinted back towards the tunnel. The beast thundered after her.

"How awful," cried Madam Grunger.

A hideous scream rang out and Madam Grunger went so pale Polly feared she'd keel over on the spot.

"Oh my," cried Inspector Rington.

"What if..." Before Polly could voice her fear smoke smouldered through the trees and the beast re-appeared, angrier than ever and this time it was heading straight for them.

The loopins screeched in alarm, heading for safety in the tops of the tallest trees. With a terrific flapping of wings the queen took to the air leading the goldicoots back to the forest leaving the Colonel battered and bruised lying in the grass.

"You can't just leave us!" cried Polly.

"Goldermare, what about the Colonel?"

The beast raised its huge wings and launched itself into the air, moving closer and closer with each powerful beat.

Mussley squeaked and burrowed under a bush. The goat bleated and bolted into the forest. Madam Grunger began to sway and Inspector Rington let out a sound like a strangled chicken.

Polly's father reached out for her. "We have to get out of here."

The Colonel was already on his feet and bounded towards them. "Scared of the beast are we?" he laughed.

Polly saw the basu monkey out of the corner of her eye. It

had scampered over to the bush where the pistol had landed and now sat on his haunches waving the pistol in the air, chattering.

"Bring it to me, that's a good boy," called Polly, beckoning the monkey as the Colonel got nearer. "There's no where to run to," said Polly when her father flashed her a questioning look.

The beast let out a terrifying screech which even made the Colonel falter.

Madam Grunger hit the ground with a terrific thud! She was out cold, with her feet pointing up to the sky. In his haste to help her, disorientated without his glasses, Inspector Rington tripped and fell by her side, bashing his head.

"Polly!" cried her father.

The beast flew over the waterfall and out across the golden pool. The basu monkey chased through the grass and up to Polly's ankles.

"Take the pistol," cried Polly.

"What the…"

The basu monkey held up the pistol to where Polly's father stood frozen.

"Just take it," urged Polly.

Polly's father grabbed hold of it and pointed it towards the Colonel just as the beast flew low overhead, its shadow throwing Polly and her father into darkness.

In that moment the Colonel cried out and lunged for Polly.

The beast swooped overhead, circling them, sticking out a long black tongue which trembled, emitting a wailing cry. There was a struggle and muffled voices. Polly's father cried out. She heard the sound of a fist against flesh then felt the Colonel's arm around her neck. She smelt his sweat in her nostrils, felt the heat of his body and the roughness of his jacket against her skin.

Frantically Polly sought to see her father, who had crumpled in pain, a bruise on his cheek, a drop of blood trickling from his nose.

"You always were weak," sneered Colonel Brisket. "Now get away from me."

The beast swept over head, circling its prey. Polly's father still held the pistol in his hand and in a panic he raised it in the air and fired.

A shot rang out.

Polly closed her eyes, her heart pounding so hard she could barely hear anything else. Opening her eyes she found herself being hauled along the wooden plank that still lay across the golden pool, her neck in an arm lock. The world span for a moment, a golden haze of sun reflected on liquid gold, the shifting face of her father, his mouth contorted into a silent scream. He was standing, the gun shaking in his hand. Wings beat above her head and acrid smoke lingered in the air. How could it have come to this?

Chapter 36

"Put that pistol down or I'll throw her in." The Colonel squeezed hold of Polly tighter still.

"I'll never trust you again," said Polly's father, his words trembling almost as much as the hand that held the pistol. "I'll shoot you, I will. Just let her go. Can't you see the beast is just biding its time, we have to get out of here now."

Polly wasn't sure what she feared most: a silent death plunging into liquid gold or being snatched by the beast. But she did know her father would never shoot his own brother, not his own blood. No, she was sure of that. There had to be another way. The beast would surely take them all, just like Premble and Pruella. Or was this all part of the goldicoot's curse, for she too had gold in her pocket, the fob that the loopins had made.

Polly watched the beast circle them as if he were toying with them, like a cat when it corners a mouse. But maybe it wasn't, maybe it was waiting, but what for? The gunshot must have scared it but a very strange thought raced through Polly's mind and the more she thought about it the more it made sense. Maybe the beast couldn't decide what to do? She remembered what her father had told her, that the Colonel had killed the beast's mate and that was why it was angry. She also remembered that day back in the maze of tunnels; the beast had allowed her to leave as though it didn't consider her a threat. Maybe, just maybe, the beast wanted revenge but Polly being there was confusing it. She just hoped Goldermare would listen to her.

"Goldermare, you have to help us."

At first Polly's plea was met with silence, then at last Polly heard her.

"We cannot attack a fellow creature of our world, it is not permitted."

Goldermare had to help, she just had to.

"But it's the Colonel who killed the beast's mate, not me or my father. Can't you tell the beast we mean no harm?"

Polly's father steadied his arm.

"One last chance, Colonel. Let Polly go, I can hit you from here, don't think I won't."

The Colonel laughed and shoved Polly so hard her left leg fell off the plank and her foot missed the molten gold by millimetres.

"I don't believe you'd risk hitting Polly and you're not that good a shot," sneered the Colonel.

Behind her, Polly heard the beating of wings. It wasn't the beast, that continued to circle them like a gull around a fishing vessel out at sea. Polly daren't move, her whole body was trembling.

Then Polly saw her, Goldermare, so small in the sky compared to the beast. She swept out across the golden pool close enough to whisper to the beast whose wings still never missed a beat.

Sweat dripped down Professor Gertram's nose. Polly heard Mussley squeak and saw him crawl out from under the bush.

Just as quickly as Goldermare had appeared so she flew away again. The beast held steady. Pulling back its wings it dived, shooting towards the Colonel and Polly like an arrow released from a bow. Polly caught her breath.

Mussley sprang towards her, leapt onto the plank and raced along it until he was by her feet. Then he lunged at the Colonel, biting him hard on the ankle, drawing deep red blood.

"Oooooooooooooow!" The Colonel jumped, letting go of Polly.

Polly took her chance and ran down the wooden plank back to firm ground, convinced the Colonel would topple over but the beast snatched him up by the scruff of the neck, carrying him high above the golden pool.

"Polly!" cried her father, running towards her, his arms outstretched.

In her father's arms Polly stopped trembling, the beating of her heart soothed by every second in his embrace. The Colonel dangled from the beast's grasp, desperately thrashing

211

from side to side until the beast loosened its grip and down fell Colonel Brisket, landing in the gold with an almighty splash!

Glug, glug, glug.

Golden bubbles rippled across the surface and he was gone.

Madam Grunger groaned and Inspector Rington sat up, rubbing his head. Polly and her father watched the beast gracefully fly far beyond the golden waterfall, soaring high above the trees until it was a little dot on the distant horizon and that too disappeared from view.

Polly's father threw the pistol into the golden pool. "It's all right everyone, the beast's gone, so too has the Colonel."

Madam Grunger let the Inspector pull her up. Mussley squeaked triumphantly and the basu monkey clapped loudly.

As if hearing his name there came a loud glug from the molten gold and up sprang the Colonel, only he looked so different in solid gold. His mouth was wide open in surprise, his arms outstretched and every hair on his body was immobilised in gold forever.

Goldermare flew over the golden pool and came to rest on the Colonel's head, like a pigeon on a statue.

Polly hugged her father, knowing that they would be leaving the Hibrodean rainforest together.

Chapter 37

With time the goldicoots' world would be back to how it was before Edmund Milner stumbled upon it. New trees would grow from the seeds the loopins had planted and the dirty scar of the mine would be no more, hidden under a new covering of grass.

On Polly's last morning the bushes were burgeoning with blossom, their delicate scent all around. The loopins were busy as ever in their workshops and the goldicoots filled the air with shimmering gold. Polly wondered how many loopins paddled canoes beneath where she sat.

Madam Grunger strapped her carpet bag to the back of the goat.

"You'll need a really good bath in carbolic soap and a hair cut when we get home. You've become wilder everyday."

Inspector Rington was helping Polly's father dismantle the mineshaft, it was the least the Inspector could do. Polly sat in the shade of a bush with Mussley. She was surprised to see a loopin scurrying towards her. She'd wanted to say goodbye but hadn't known how. The gold fob still lay in her pinafore pocket, now she took it out and held it up.

"Thank you," she said.

The loopin crouched down beside her and with its small blue hand it closed Polly's fingers around the fob. Did it mean for her to keep it? "But it belongs to you," said Polly, hoping the loopin understood.

The loopin smiled and made a shrill cry that Polly had no hope of understanding. The loopin held out a bracelet of emeralds and carefully secured it around Polly's wrist. It was the most beautiful present Polly had ever been given. Then the loopin scampered away leaving Polly with a lump in her throat and no idea what to say.

"Oh Mussley." She hugged him tightly and held him up to her face. "I can't wait to show you my home."

"Surely you're not thinking of taking that animal with us?" Madam Grunger lowered herself onto the grass under the shade of her now very shabby umbrella. "He belongs here, with the basu monkey. I really don't think…"

Mussley squeaked loudly and wrapped himself around Polly's shoulders and there he stayed until Madam Grunger dozed off in the sun. Polly left her to snore and set off in search of the queen of the goldicoots.

Entering the royal palace it seemed such a different place. Goldicoots flew in and around, through the archways and along the balconies. They perched on the balustrades and nested in the alcoves. Polly looked down at the grave marked with a gold cross beside the tree. Polly had helped her father bury the brave goldicoots who had given their lives for their queen.

Polly climbed the golden staircase. The goldicoot queen

perched high on a balcony, watching Polly as she climbed closer.

"Your Majesty." Polly wasn't sure how she should address a queen but it seemed fitting. "It's been an honour to meet you. I'm so very sorry for... what happened."

The queen blinked her emerald eyes and flicked her turquoise plume.

"You are always welcome here. Maybe one day you will return. There are many worlds to see. I'm sure the loopins would guide you."

Polly nodded. She'd not told her father about the loopins' secret and for now at least she'd done all the exploring she wanted.

"Time we were going, Polly."

Polly's father stood below at the bottom of the staircase.

"Coming," called Polly. "But I have to find Goldermare before we leave."

Polly raced down the staircase and out into the forest, running alongside her father.

"She's waiting for us beside the golden pool." There was a sparkle in her father's eye.

"What is it?" He obviously knew something she didn't.

"Wait and see. You're not the only one who talks to Goldermare you know. I just didn't want the Colonel to know."

How silly of her. In all the excitement Polly had forgotten that it had been Goldermare that had helped her father and left the fob for Polly to discover. If it hadn't been for Goldermare, Polly would never have found her father again and the Colonel...well that didn't bear thinking about any longer.

Goldermare stood beside the golden pool and beside her a small ball of brown fluff played by her feet. Polly watched the baby bird wobble its first steps and flap its wings as yet too small and incapable of flight. Or course...Polly remembered the golden egg that sat in the nest in the tunnel. It must have hatched.

Goldermare encouraged her baby to dip its beak into the golden pool. Polly watched in amazement. As the baby goldicoot drank the molten gold its fluffy brown feathers turned to sparkling gold, like a golden powder puff with legs.

"We'll miss you," said Polly.

"You are brave and wise. We are proud to call you one of us."

Chapter 38

16ᵗʰ September 1897

*The bird rescue centre will officially open tomorrow. I've
painted the sign and sent out invitations. Father and I
are delighted that we have been able to take in so many
injured and abandoned birds. My favourite has to be
Jasper, the Adrianne parrot, whose broken wing means
he will never fly again but his language would shock
Madam Grunger.*

Polly blotted her diary entry dry and admired the emerald ink
that father had given her as a present on her birthday. She sat
in her father's chair, the green leather was cracked and her
feet still didn't reach the floor. Mussley sat on the armrest and
squeaked his approval. The basu monkey sat high on a shelf
where he clapped enthusiastically. The goat peered in through
the window.

The glass domes of stuffed birds were long since gone and
in their place stood books, every book about birds and
animals she and her father could find in Wiggington along
with a vast array of maps. Many covered regions unexplored
by any zoologists. And of course her father's journal of the
Hibrodean rainforest lay there too along with that of Edmund
Milner, which they had had bound in leather.

Polly didn't miss Madam Grunger one bit, even though

her father said it wasn't polite to say so. She was due to be married to Inspector Rington at the end of next month and Polly was to be their bridesmaid. Madam Grunger made a point of reminding Polly she'd have no pearls to wear.

Inspector Rington's promotion to Chief Constable meant they could afford a town house in Wiggington and Polly was invited to go for afternoon tea once a month for fish paste sandwiches and fruit scones on the condition that she didn't bring Mussley.

Polly's father had never been permitted back into the Royal Ornithological Society. After all, those who chased mythological birds were not worthy of membership. But Polly and her father did visit the National History Museum regularly. They liked to visit the golden feather, still displayed as 'species unknown'. It made them smile. They were the only ones who knew the goldicoots not only existed but thrived beneath the Hibrodean rainforest but of course they would never tell.

Poor Mundle never quite recovered and was moved to the coast in the hope that bracing sea air might aid his recovery. But Polly knew some people never recovered from an encounter with a beast.

As their carriage passed the road where the city zoo once stood, its red brick wall had been demolished along with the zoo. Pruella Trimbleton had no relatives and no one would have wanted her debts anyway. The site was for sale as an excellent plot for town houses and maybe a shop or two.

Upstairs in Polly's bedroom she sat on the floor under the window. There the doll's house still stood but she'd cleared out the dust under the roof and re-homed the spider. In its place sat a small wooden box and inside that the golden fob. Polly took it out. She opened its case and watched the tiny gold dials tremble and wondered where the loopins were now.

THE END

Dawn Treacher

Dawn Treacher lives in North Yorkshire with her husband, daughter and a cat called Florrie. This story and many others were penned in Geraldine, her caravan in the garden.

Printed in Great Britain
by Amazon

47878059R00135